Thank you to everyone who supported our Kickstarter to bring our first two anthologies to life!

Special thanks to:

Ryan
Shoni, Nathan, Zavary & Quillan
Tobias
James B.
Julie Bozza
Gina Marie Byars
Cathy Caravan
Marianne and Bob Caravan
Anne Cartwright
Aisha Cissna & Juan Cervantes
Gabriel di Chiara
Caz and David Field
Natasha Lopez
Lauren Perruzza
Ashley Pitre
Reena T
Alva Tang

CONTENTS

THE KNOT WOUND ROUND YOUR FINGER

AN ANTHOLOGY ON MEMORY, HISTORY & INHERITANCE

Edited by Devon Field

bell press
anthologies

ISBN 978-0-9948127-2-8 (print) | ISBN 978-0-9948127-4-2 (ebook)

Cover and text design by Angela Caravan
Copyediting by Devon Field
Note on the spelling: as this is an international anthology, regional spelling choices of each author have been maintained

Printed and bound in Canada

LIBRARY AND ARCHIVES CANADA CATALOGUING IN PUBLICATION
Title: The knot wound round your finger : an anthology on memory, history & inheritance.
Identifiers: Canadiana (print) 20210331569 | Canadiana (ebook) 20210332107 | ISBN 9780994812728
  (softcover) | ISBN 9780994812742 (HTML)
Subjects: LCSH: Literature, Modern—21st century. | LCSH: Memory—Literary collections.
Classification: LCC PR1151 .K66 2021 | DDC 820.8/0353—dc23

INTRODUCTION

I came to the theme of this anthology through my interest in history. Over the last number of years, history has increasingly become the focus of my reading and writing, particularly medieval history and the stories of its travellers, both real and fabricated, its Ruy Gonzalez de Clavijos and its John Mandevilles, its narratives that blended first-hand experience with borrowed reports and repeated fictions. There's no great leap from that interest to the topic of memory: how we preserve it and hand it down, how we use or distort it, and how it informs who we are both socially and individually. I thought it sounded like a good theme for an anthology.

There is so much that can be made of the topic of memories, so many different possibilities to explore, and I've been delighted to see what this group of authors have done with it. From speculative-fiction to memoir, the fiction and non-fiction pieces in this anthology demonstrate a wonderful variety of approaches to the theme.

How are memories made? Can we trust them? How do they make us? How do we engage with our family histories and the surprises, discomforts, and traumas they may bring? How can we live in a healthy relationship with our past? How might future innovations bring new ways to interact with that past, to recover, fabricate, or recreate it, to maybe change ourselves in the process? The authors whose work was chosen for this collection engage with all of these questions with heart, humour, and thoughtful reflection, and I could not be more proud of them. I hope you enjoy reading these as much as I have.

As you're reading, you might notice some divergent spelling from piece to piece. These authors do not all come from one place, and there is not only one written English. I elected to follow that of the author in each case.

Devon Field, editor

A PHOTOGRAPH OF MY MOTHER

by Emma Prior

In 1958, Grandad stole my mother. I know, *stole* might be too strong a word, but from where I'm standing, what took place was theft. Sure, his marriage had broken down, the love between husband and wife as dry as sand. But now I'm a mother myself, I can't begin to think how he persuaded himself to remove a child from her mother and set up home on the other side of the world.

In some ways the theft was made easy for him, like plotting a route on a classroom map of the world with pins and string. Start in one corner of the Empire. Board the ship with a suitcase, a passport, and a child. Singapore melting into the horizon behind. Ahead, Sri Lanka, India, the Suez Canal, Egypt, the Straits of Gibraltar. Then at last, England, cold England, where new memories would be made in muted, wintery colours.

What does my mother remember of her early years beneath the equatorial sun? She's tried to fill in some gaps for me, of a culture that's in my DNA but not in my memories. Mango harvests. Christmas on the beach. Tiger Balm. Chopsticks and Chinese New Year. Joss sticks and red envelopes,

3

bank notes tucked carefully inside. Chickens in the back garden, jungle beyond that. I've thought about her memories so long and hard they've almost become my own.

She has just one photo of her childhood, a black and white one, curled at the edges, taken outside the house she left behind. The image is imprinted in my mind as if I were the photographer, peering through the lens in the sweltering heat. She's a snip of a girl, in her Sunday best dress, lace-topped ankle socks, white bow clipped into her black hair. A neat little row of teeth peeping out from a tight, cautious smile. My mother as a child, captured in a single image, her whole life stretched out ahead of her, like the journey she was about to take. Or is it me I see, or perhaps even my own daughter? The three of us meld together. We will share what history we have, and the future is a journey we will take together.

Emma Prior lives in Liverpool where she runs grassroots, community-building projects. Her writing has been published in several independent anthologies, and she's currently working on her first novel. Twitter: @emmavprior

THE LIBRARY

by Ibrahim Babátúndé Ibrahim

Much of my memories from my secondary school days are vague, like a framed picture clouded by layers of dust on the strip of glass behind which it sits. But there are also the parts that are still as vivid as immersive 3D clips. I suppose it's the same for everyone. There must be those memories that sit just beyond a trigger of thoughts, experiences raw enough to still tune your feelings like AM/FM radio, flashes that take you back to the exact emotions that shaped those particular moments.

Of these vivid memories, there are ones to forget just as there are others to cherish. Anyone who attended a Nigerian Federal Government College in the '90s can tell you about hostel life: wicked seniors, 'A Boy' errand calls, maggot-making toilets, Saturday morning inspections, (hard) labour days, visiting day heartbreaks, and general homesickness. But there were also the social nights, dining hall blues, inter-house sports, good vibes with special friends, occasional side-chat with your smitten crush, and last-night food marathons.

My life was a steady boat floating upon a gentle stream until the chaos of boarding school happened. I wasn't ready for the waves. It felt as though I was drowning from the first day, wandering around in a sea of other students wearing house-wear of pink shirts and blue trousers like me, unable to steady my thoughts as the flock dragged me this way and that with every ring of the bell, appearance of a teacher, or scream of a senior.

The morning after my arrival, I went in search of the senior I had been assigned to, so he could come bath me. I was eleven and had never bathed myself at this time. He must have been super-irritated because his rough palm assaulted my face as though I had asked him to clean up my vomit. This was no fairy-tale, and as much as I had always longed to be away from the seeming 'boringness' of home, every drop of tear down my face that morning prayed to go back there.

I had never been as close to the whip as I was here. It was out tormenting me at the slightest provocation—sometimes, for no reason. Once, it was for mispronouncing a 'gentle' senior's name. Another time, it was for not running away when a 'wicked' one appeared. The whip woke us up every morning, chased us to the dining hall for every meal. Heck, the whip even crashed without mercy if one was found not to have visited the mosque or church for prayers.

My confidence had been badly shaken, and my esteem was in tatters. The hostel felt like a refugee camp and the school compound like a prison yard. I had believed that coming off primary school as a frequent first-position student, I could find some solace in class, but class also proved to offer no comfort. The first-position student thing was a mirage here. Teachers were just as mean with the whip as the seniors, and the students who put down names of noise-makers only seemed to write names of those outside of their cliques.

The tidal waves of these deep-end waters had me off balance for a long time. I can actually say that I never really steadied my boat in there, but I would soon understand the system enough to go with its flow without tipping over. When I began to steal away to a secret spot to dive into the different worlds in my novels, it was my way of learning to find music in the system's chaotic rhythm. The problem was, I had read every single one I had and was only re-reading. Whenever I didn't feel like reading, I'd scribble in my diary, usually about the beating I got from the seniors in the hostel, or how the teachers and class were no better, or just how sick I was of the place, dying to go back home to the loving warmth of my parents and siblings.

One of the first entries I intended for my diary that wasn't a sad event was my first social night experience. When it was announced, I wasn't sure what to expect. They'd said it was for some entertainment, but whenever the seniors gathered us up for beating, they'd always called it the same name. My heart pounded in my chest as I made my way to the assembly hall after dinner.

Walking into the hall as confused as the other new students in the crowd, the first thing that struck differently were the bright, blinking lights. Next, I noticed it was the voices of students and not teachers over the microphone. Soon after, the strong and commanding sound of very loud, sweet music rent the air. The melodies felt as though the skies had opened up and were raining down torrents of confetti. My soul was drenched in it, lifted off its usual gloom.

My dance must have been so vigorous that the straps on my sandal ripped in two different places by the time the lights went out. My feet ached like they had just survived a marathon, but as I slid into my tiny space between three of my friends on our hard, pressed mattress, not knowing what shoes I would be wearing to class the next morning, I closed my eyes to the flurry of words stringing together in preparation for a glorious entry into my diary at the earliest opportunity.

The next day, I was sitting at my table in the dining hall before dawn had fully melted into morning. Most students were just waking up and heading out to get water for their bath. I had walked with only one foot of my sandals strapped. The straps on the other were still ripped, but I didn't want to be caught walking barefooted to breakfast. This, however, meant that I had left my morning duty undone. This act was unpardonable to the seniors, and I knew I had to find a way to get it done before classes were over.

Everyone flocked from the dining hall to their respective classrooms after breakfast, everyone except me. I had slid under the table and waited for the hall to clear out before resurfacing. My school uniform of white shirt over white trousers was clean (though not pressed), and I had my school bag hugging me from behind, but down below, I only had a foot of sandal on.

"Are you not going to class?" said a female voice from behind me.

Lot's wife from the Bible could not have frozen any stiffer than I did.

The owner of the voice came around to stand before me. It was Ayo, a senior prefect. She looked immaculate in her iron-pressed green pinafore over a sparkling white shirt. Her white socks and polished Cortina shoes made me feel somewhat inadequate. Her big eyes travelled from my face down to my feet and rested there.

"What happened to your sandals?"

"Social night…" I managed, scarcely moving my mouth.

Her low laugh ended in a coughing fit. I wanted to say sorry and offer a hand, but I was still pretty much locked on the same spot.

After she'd stopped coughing, she steadied herself, adjusted her beret, and asked, "What class are you?"

"I'm in JSS1, ma."

"I'm not a 'ma.' My name is Ayo. I take it you don't want your class girls seeing you barefooted and laughing at you. I know someone who can fix the sandal. I also know a route where no-one will be looking or laughing. I'm actually going that way."

The route was the ring road that encircled the main area of the school, including the dining and assembly halls, the classrooms, the boys' and girls' hostels, the administrative block, and a section of the staff quarters. I walked with one foot strapped and the other bare, listening to Ayo talk, offering very little in exchange. Even when we walked past my secret reading spot, as it was along this route, I claimed no familiarity.

Tall trees lined both sides of the road. Their branches formed a canopy above us, and their fallen leaves carpeted most of the way. Soon, we approached an area that was truly unfamiliar. Ayo stopped by a footpath and asked me to hand over the bad sandal.

"Being found outside of your classroom at this time will attract a beating. Go and wait in the library. No one will question you there," she said, pointing to a white building off a different footpath.

The only library I had ever been in was the one-shelf one that housed my dad's books back home. My thoughts, as I made my way to the building, were on why anyone needed such a big place to house one or two shelves. There were a number of steps to get to the long corridor that stretched for the entire length of the building. I climbed and then stopped by a door marked 'entrance.'

The first thing that hit me was the smell of processed wood, books new and old. I took a few steps in and beheld the towering racks filling up a large part of the massive hall. Books of different sizes peeked from them, with a rainbow of book covers and a galaxy of fonts. My eyes bulged, and a gasp escaped my throat. My heart skipped and then rose, giving me that jumpy feeling you get when you're driven over a hilly part in a speeding car. An attendant was talking to me, helping me store away my bag and showing me how to navigate the sections, but I had been consumed by a welling from deep within and I hardly heard a word he said.

As soon as I was alone, I was running my fingers across the stacks, feeling the hardness of the pages without opening the books yet. The walls had fallen away, and the sun shone directly into the space. The racks were giant trees, and the books were their rich, colourful leaves. Federal Government College Ilorin was a distant reality; I was in a different place now.

Cover after cover caught my attention. Then, seeing that the different fields housed by each rack were arranged in alphabetical order, I decided to survey them starting from letter A. So, I went from 'Architecture, Art, Agricultural Science' to 'Biology, Bio-Science, Botany' and past C, D, E, until I arrived at 'L, Literature.'

There were all kinds of novels. I saw popular fairy-tales in glossy hardbacks, big photo-books that looked like photo albums, thin and bulky books, dogeared and new books, books with colourful covers and with bland ones, some with long sentences as titles and others with as short as two letters and an exclamation mark.

I decided to start with one book and see how many I could read before my time there was up. I settled in at the bottom layer of the rack marked 'Literature,' kicked off my lone sandal, and was soon tumbling down a rabbit hole with Alice in her Wonderland adventures.

Time ceased to exist as I sped through page after page, and book after book. I knew there were other people in the library, but I could see, hear, smell, or feel nothing else if it was not on a page I was reading. When my buttocks began to feel sore, I adjusted and rested on one arm, and then I shifted to the other arm. Soon, I laid on my back, and then turned over with my legs hanging over my buttocks. My stomach rumbled but I did not hear it. I yawned many a time, but I wasn't conscious of any.

I could feel my body shutting down, but my brain could not be pulled from the words it was ingesting. There was a general blur, and then as though the universe was wired to my system, the lights snapped off. Distant croaks and chirps floated into my ears as everything came rushing back: the attendant, the library, Ayo and my sandal, classes, dining hall, my undone morning duty, roll calls, lights out, whipping!

I stood up from the bottom of the rack and felt my way out of the section to the reading area. The moon shone through the windows and cast long shadows of the tables and chairs inwards.

What was the time? How long had I been there? Ayo and the attendant must have looked for me—how did I not hear them? Most of all, I had missed lights out and knew how much trouble I could be in—why was I not alarmed?

I stood by a window and looked back at the giant racks, each one reaching from the floor to the ceiling, all pregnant with books. I closed my eyes and sniffed in the strong, intoxicating smell of the different kinds of paper that filled the room. My lips parted into a big smile as I was reminded of all the positive emotions struggling for space in my heart, and just why alarm could not have room at this time.

The night was long and dark, but I still crawled my way around until I found the shelf that held my bag, unzipped it, and fetched my diary.

With the moon for company, I sat by the window and poured words of my most joyful day so far at Federal Government College Ilorin onto my diary. The words came alive as I spilled them, and it was once again social night, but in the library, with the confetti shower and thumping melodies among the trees of racks and leaves of books, the moon shining with the sun's glory down on the space, and me showing off different dance steps like no one was watching.

This was until the DJ scratched the music to a stop, to change songs perhaps. But someone was then saying: "Is that not his sandal?"

"Oh, that's the other foot of the sandals quite alright." The answer was from Ayo's voice.

I opened my eyes, and the sun shining in through the window forced me to shut them back for a few seconds. So much awaited me today, but for now, it was a bright, beautiful morning.

"The Library" previously appeared in Chaffin Journal.

Ibrahim Babátúndé Ibrahim took 20 years to find his way back to his passion after he was forcibly sent to science class in high school. In 2019, he left a successful ten-year career in media & entertainment to become a writer.

Since that time, his work has been accepted for publication in *JMWW*, *Door is a Jar Magazine*, *Ake Review*, *Agbowó Magazine*, *Landlocked Magazine*, *The Chaffin Journal*, *The Decolonial Passage*, and more. He finished as a finalist in Goge Africa's #GogeAfrica20 Writing Contest, and *Ibua Journal*'s Packlight Series. He was longlisted for the 2020 Dzanc Diverse Voices Prize. He has also been nominated for the Pushcart Prize.

Ibrahim's work explores the human experience from an African perspective. He's @heemthewriter across social media.

TEA BREAK

by Shereen Hussain

Sadia was reading a book about the East India Company and how it was given the biggest corporate bailout the world would ever know. This same corporation would cause a domino effect of destruction and exploitation. An entire heritage would be erased, beginning a cycle of generational trauma and self-loathing.Sadia stared at the steam emitting from her cup. Had it really all begun with this harmless beverage that she consumed daily? Sadia remembered a tea party at her cousin Huma's house.

The temperatures are so high that they can smell the heat. But everyone craves that treacherous tea regardless. Wise elders know how chai drinking has a cooling effect through perspiration. The colonials take this secret back to England with their jewels and even learn of a meal called High Tea. Mini kebabs, dainty colonized cucumber sandwiches, crunchy samosas, and fish cutlets. All served on china with a pink rose design.

The younger children want the adults to speed up the ceremony as they beg for a water fight. This was light years before Nerf guns or Super Soakers. Sadia's mother would fill up the water tank and all would grab jugs or saucepans. Uncle Khalid would take one last gulp of chai and begin to tell stories about pranks from his youth until it was time for everyone to call for rickshaws and bid the evening farewell.

In India, it is as though the whole year revolves around the monsoon season. Rain is not an encumbrance or an annoyance. There is no reaching for umbrellas or wellington boots. Here they pray for precipitation. When the clouds send forth their aquatic bounty, the streets are filled with children. Huma and Kamal tear out pages from the previous day's Hyderabad Times *and quickly construct paper boats for racing. Razia and Rana simply dance and rejoice in the God-given downpour. Once they are drenched, they walk home in muddy streets to warm baths and mild scoldings.*

Then, when the showery season subsides, it will be time for the annual zoo picnic. The Ahmed men are wannabe moghuls. For them, it is less about seeing the animals and more about the food.

Naturally, everyone eagerly awaits the arrival of Hasina Aunty. She is always three hours late but brings the best lunch. Perfectly spherical shami kebabs and parathas of exactly the right thickness. Then metallic dabbah upon dabbah of dals, chutneys, and khorma. Uncle Khalid has never actually seen these world-famous zoological gardens. He has missed out on the rare Asian lion, a unique snow-colored Bengal tiger, the sloth bear, and over a hundred species of unusual birds in the expansive aviary. He is blissfully unaware of the chattering hyenas as well as the king cobra in the huge herpetology collection. Uncle Khalid simply lies down in the grassed-in eating area where even the peacocks leave him alone to snore contentedly until it is time to go home.

Sadia put down her cup, and her thoughts turned to the day she came home from school to see her grandmother throwing belongings into a blanket. They could hear the sound of gunshots in the background heralding the arrival of the British army. Soon after, Grandmother covered Sadia's mouth as she screamed while they all watched Uncle Khalid being dragged away by soldiers.

No one in Sadia's family had spoken a word against the British to this day. They had never named their past nor their pain. They accepted that they had been given the gift of the English language, a job, and a British passport.

Sadia threw her half-empty teacup against the wall. As the ceramic shards fell everywhere, Sadia ran to pick them up, black tea dregs mingling with the blood dripping from her hand.

Shereen Hussain was born in India and raised in the U.K., but later moved to California. She has a degree in French and English Literature from the University of London and one in Education from San Francisco State University. Shereen was a teacher for many years and then entered the field of international business. However, writing has been a lifelong passion.

Her short stories have been published by *Freedom Voices* in San Francisco, *Lascaux Review*, and by a publisher in the U.K. Her play, *Inventing the Truth* has been performed in a high school in California and a community theater in Illinois. It is about the invention of the ice cream cone by a Syrian immigrant.

VIOLENCE IN THE CALM

by NC Hernandez

I should say something here about beginnings, and how I don't believe in them. I should tell you that beginnings are relative; one person's beginning is another's middle, or ending. But the truth is that I was too late. I had planned on traveling back to the places of my youth with my abuelo Rafael, on the dirt roads of La Calma where I, a pubescent youth, learned to drive a stick shift while dodging roosters, where I asked an uncle how old I had to be to drive on the paved city streets and he responded, *Old enough to see over the steering wheel.* I made so many grand plans when still that young man; then my abuelo got cancer. I was too broke to afford the ticket and too proud to ask him to pay my way, and just like that, he was too ill to travel, then he was dead. The painful irony was that it took his death for us to travel to Guadalajara together. His ending was my beginning.

The year after he died, my finances stabilized enough to start making yearly sojourns back to Mexico. Then I began to go every four months. I had heard from aunts and uncles the story of a gruesome triple murder in the family that happened when my abuelo was still a young man himself, but then my uncle Jeff told me that the two child survivors, Ernesto and

Victoria, were still alive in La Calma. I was not going to miss this chance again, so I told him that I needed a liaison, someone who had known these elder relatives since childhood, and to meet me in Guadalajara. I jumped on a plane and took a house in the nearby zona Chapalita with space for my uncle to sleep and for me to write.

The first place that Jeff and I went was to see my eighty-three-year-old great aunt Victoria, Ernesto's older sister, about the murders. Knowing that many of the older generation in my family don't care to discuss the past, or relive the pain, I had asked Jeff if we could communicate with them well ahead of the trip and make arrangements to conduct interviews.

Nah, Jeff said, *That's not how you do it, ey, you just have to say you're coming to visit, because if you say you want to interview them, they'll just say no.*

After a series of pleasantries and light conversation, Victoria immediately said no, and that it was still too painful to speak about the murders. I could tell my questions had transported her back to that same day. I could see my abuelo's face in hers—the side of the family I don't look like—with the same grimace he had on his deathbed. Fleas bit at my ankles while she diverted the conversation to her sons' banda group, and their prize-winning cocks in cages behind the house. The open door was the sole source of light that collapsed on the cement floor in a sunlit rectangle. I sat back in my chair and angled my notebook to block the reflection while Jeff persisted with the oblique questions, each met with the steadfast diversion of a politician. I hadn't seen Ernesto or Victoria since I was a child, but I began to worry that this trip was going to be another missed opportunity.

I asked Victoria if I could take her photograph, and raised the Leica IIIf to my eye. The year of the murder that took her mother and siblings, a still reconstructing Germany sent this little camera to the US as part of its export market, and there it stayed for sixty years before I found it and brought it to La Calma, exposing this visage of trauma onto tiny Japanese celluloid strips. I could feel that there were too many countries in her tiny room, and she did not want to talk to us, so I left Victoria's casita feeling dejected, but Jeff was confident that Ernesto would talk to us. Once on the street, I checked my socks for fleas and looked at the nearly blank page in my notebook where the words *Cockfighter* and *No Luck* were scrawled across its surface. We flagged a white and yellow taxi that was freshly painted, contrasting the faded hues of the buildings, and we rode from the south side of La Calma to the north, dust rising behind our tires into the orange light of the midday sun. The same sun that barely lit Victoria's house minutes ago was now blinding me and enveloping the street in its strange frequencies.

La Calma has changed a lot since the 1940s. Dirt roads have been exchanged for paved ones, but there was apparently nowhere for the forgotten dust to settle except back down, and so it mingles with the gravel until they are indistinguishable from one another. The buzz of the highway connects La Calma to the remainder of Guadalajara, which has now swallowed the area and relabelled it a neighborhood of the city. It is where my abuelo on his own La Calma property once dragged a pitbull to the back of his house and shot it with his revolver because it bit me in the face.

When Jeff and I got to Ernesto's house, a cold stillness emanated from the walls of the windowless room we sat in, and like a cave, the light from this single door shone on Ernesto's face. The baby blue in Ernesto's loose-fitting plaid shirt matched the color of his walls, and bits of white hair clung to the edges of his head. Framed photographs of relatives, mostly dead, lined the upper part of the walls of the tile-floored living room, and the changing of the faces passed my eyes like a zoetrope as I spun on my heels from the center. Everywhere I looked, he was surrounded in this house by dusty memories. Ernesto sat with his right leg flung back; it has barely worked since he was shot in the hip, and it is now shorter than the other. He wears one boot with a large sole and heel to compensate for the difference in length, much of it obscured by the floor-scraping bootcut of his blue worker's pants. I wondered if Victoria would consider this a betrayal, and remembered that I hadn't asked her if she wanted the tale untold or just didn't want to do the telling. Ernesto bounced his two-year-old grandson on his good leg and spoke plainly about ancient and horrific violence, unbearable pains, eternal losses.

It is a strange thing to travel back to this place in Mexico where it began, or at least where it began for me. Ernesto Vazquez sat on the arm of a small sofa, towering over me as I scrawled in my notebook. I felt both like an intruder and a relative as I tried not to miss a word the old man said. Nearly seventy years after the violence I came to ask him about, I sensed that even the small privileges I had in California were, no matter how obscure, magnified here, and partly a result of his life. Ernesto is one of the oldest members of my family—my grandfather's nephew—and I went to him to uncover this earliest known family tragedy in the hope of finding some connection to the violence that seemed to follow us across borders and time. After the murder of my eldest cousin in 2016 in southern California, I started seeking out the root cause of violence in my family. Every time I thought I had landed on it, I realized I had only turned back another layer, and there was still further to dig, more of ourselves to uncover. I needed a beginning.

I just heard a scream, I didn't know what it was about, Ernesto said. I could tell that it had been many years since he had told this story to anyone. I could feel time slip back to his childhood, decades before I was born, to the day he had climbed a small hill above the entrance gate to the rancho to tie up the horses and had just entered the granary when he heard several shots. I wondered about the ethics of bringing him back to his original experience of violence, but my ruminations were cut short when Ernesto startled me, yelling out, *PAH-PAH, just shots and shots!* Ernesto began with no detectable anger in his words, no sense of deprivation over this event that happened almost seventy years ago and consumed half of his life searching for the killer that also shot him. On that day in 1951, Juan Limón shot Ernesto's brother Juan twice, the first bullet hitting him in the right shoulder and the second hitting him in the back as he turned to run. It was only centimeters from his heart. Juan held his wounds and left a trail of blood behind him as he ran with his sister Victoria through the main gate of the ranch and into the corn fields to escape, collapsing close-by and bleeding out.

Juan Limón's brother was married to Ernesto's aunt Margarita, but Ernesto does not refer to Juan Limón, another of La Calma's campesinos, as anything but *my uncle's brother*, or *that man*. Ernesto believed that the trouble on the day of the murders had started when his mother, Maria de Jesus, asked Juan Limón if he would tie up his pig because it was destroying the crops on her father's parcel of land that everyone called La Trompita. During this time in Mexico, it was seen as offensive for a woman to speak to a man bluntly, and Juan Limón got angry despite Maria de Jesus speaking to him in a manner that Ernesto calls buenas palabras. Ernesto had forgotten about it in the hours that passed, until he heard the shots from the granary. Incredulous, I later asked my mother what she recalled having heard about the event. She remembered the story being that Maria de Jesus was rough, like her brother Rafael, and even that she had cursed at Juan Limón over the damage to La Trompita, but this is not how Ernesto recalls it. I felt myself invested in Ernesto's version of events at the time of the telling, forgiving any obvious biases, and understanding that memory is a fluid thing that drains through our minds and into our bodies, that it never really washes away, it just changes form. The questions I had were less about veracity anyhow, and more about inheritance. Ernesto's crippled hip and giant boot were already a brutal testimony of how violence changes us, absorbs into us, is passed out into the world in different forms.

He had that limp, but he could really dance, my mother told me. At family functions, the little nieces would line up to dance with him because he knew all the steps. He would stoop his tall frame over to dance with my mother when she was a child and lived in the larger neighboring pueblo of Zapopan. Ernesto now uses a cane, and his steps seem unsure at times, but as a young man he spent some time in La Puente, California, putting up fences for his uncle Rafael's crew.

When a new worker made a wager that he could haul a rolled bundle of chain link on his shoulder for ten yards, a feat normally requiring two men, Rafael said, *I'll bet you $50 dollars you can't carry the fence as far as Ernesto can.*

The man laughed, *But he's crippled.*

He's my strongest worker, Rafael replied.

The man kept laughing as he carried his bundle ten yards, nearly stumbling at the end; Ernesto carried the same bundle thirty yards, limping the whole way.

Ernesto worked as a driver for decades. Even a career change to law enforcement could not pull him away from the easy money of driving, and by the mid-1960s, he would drive by day—deliveries, passengers—and moonlight as a cop by night. He still keeps his cell phone and pen in his shirt pocket, ready to take down delivery orders and schedule pick-ups and drop-offs on the ruled sheets of the clipboard that he keeps by his side. He now owns his house in La Calma where he lives with his wife of sixty years along with their son, daughter-in-law, four grandchildren, one dog, and a brood of hens in the dirt lot behind the house, and when they go out in Ernesto's SUV, he insists on driving.

I look at Ernesto sitting on the arm of the sofa and see a gentleman gunslinger from the old world, a relic in the cartel-laden modernity of Mexico. He is la llora in the heart of a revolutionary Mexico that had just traded its shackles for promises of reform. The first shots of the Cristero Rebellion that began in Guadalajara, in 1926, were fired less than an hour's walk from La Calma. Before that, revolutionary violence killed 10 percent of Mexico's population between 1910 and 1920. The roar from the cannons of war continued to rattle down the halls of time well into Ernesto's generation, well into mine. His father's generation fought those wars, and he grew up with the scars. That anterior world, built and fought for by the campesinos to benefit other men, also birthed Ernesto; it was his inheritance. By staying in his traditional home, he found a corner of Guadalajara where poverty forced commerce to forfeit the march toward the future, and the development stopped on the other side of the highway that separates Zapopan from La Calma, where time stands still. Only a few miles past the line of demarcation is Plaza del Sol, Mexico's shopping capital.

•

After Ernesto heard the gun fire several times, he heard someone yell, *He got shot!* When Ernesto yelled down the hill from the granary to ask who got hit, the voice called out that it was his brother Juan. The twelve-year-old Ernesto grabbed a .38 pistol that was in the granary and ran down the hill towards the commotion by the main gate. His mother had tried to intervene, and Ernesto arrived in time to see Juan Limón shoot her two times in her swollen stomach. He stood frozen looking at his mother on the floor, not moving, and he was unable to pull the trigger and shoot Juan Limón. I feel that this is the moment that haunted him most of all, not just because it has haunted me since he told me, and not just because of the murder of his mother and unborn sibling, but because of his inability to react. He, like many of the men in my family, is unforgiving of his child self. It is here where these images, of the child and the man, collapse in my mind, flattening time as they do. I picture my cousin Nene in La Puente, lying in his own pool of blood, and I imagine my child self there with him, armed and unable to fire back at his killers.

Juan Limón turned his gun in Ernesto's direction. He put the gun right into Ernesto's belly button. Ernesto's voice shot up as he said, *Puro ombligo!*, ringing out the final *O* and putting his finger into his belly button until I could feel a phantom of the barrel in my own belly.

That's when I turned and he got me right here, Ernesto said, pointing to his left hip. The shot broke his pelvis, ringing through his midsection as his mother and her unborn child lay dying by his side, their blood mixing with his, turning grey in the soil. By this time, Juan lay dead in his sister Victoria's arms just outside the gates. Juan Limón may have thought that Ernesto would soon be dead too, so he left La Calma, knowing reprisals were going to be swift and violent from the other campesinos, especially from Rafael. Doctors later told Ernesto he would never walk again, and at one point, they wanted to amputate, but in the end his leg was left intact, but not unscathed.

Rafael showed up shortly after the shooting and was in a belligerent rage when he found out his sister and nephew had been killed. In fury, he destroyed a chain link fence, then got a gun and mounted his horse to look for Juan Limón, but the people of La Calma who had seen him escape into a sugar cane plantation were telling Rafael not to go in there. *He will see you*, people told him, *He is going to hear the horse, and he is going to shoot you.* Rafael cursed them and rode into the field on horseback, pistol in hand, searching for Juan Limón, despite the warnings. This was the last image Ernesto saw before passing out from the pain. Rafael and Juan Limón never came face to face in the sugarcane field that day, and the longer search began.

•

Ernesto has watched the pastoral times exit this world, but much of La Calma remains the same, immune to the passage of time. People still keep guard dogs on the roofs of their houses like watchtower sentinels, in the same houses they grew up in, that their parents grew up in, and that their grandparents bought as land parcels after spending their lives working that same land. The same arrangements from a hundred years ago, probably earlier: dogs upstairs, people downstairs. The residents of La Calma still know exactly and personally who to call in the neighborhood if something needs fixing, or mending, or delivering, or anything else.

The Mexican campesinos of the 1940s and 1950s were still largely existing in feudal-like circumstances, sharecropping on a landowner's land, getting what few pesos they could, and even those meager wages went directly to the patriarch of the family as was traditionally done.

You would give him all of your money and he would say, Here, have a Coke . . . You worked all day for a Coke! Ernesto said with a laugh, and with no resentment in his voice.

Schooling was barely an option for the campesinos, and Ernesto began working on the ranch as a young boy, growing maize and raising animals. His father was the patrón of the rancho for the Aviña family, and there were many resentments among the other campesinos over perceived privileges the Vazquez family must have been receiving, but the opposite was true for the children, and Ernesto's father regularly pushed him and his siblings to work even harder than the others to set an example and appear deserving of the responsibility entrusted to them. After the murders, Ernesto was left in La Calma with only his father and older sister Victoria, the casita feeling empty without the sound of his mother cooking or his brother telling jokes. Ernesto saw his father as cruel in the tender period that the family should have spent grieving together, spent focusing on Ernesto's physical recovery.

Ernesto looked at me with child's eyes and said, *I wasn't grown yet, I still didn't know what to do.* Once again I imagined myself frozen, standing next to Nene's body, the dust caking on my skin.

Without anyone to console him after the death of his mother, Ernesto began idling, drifting, getting into small teenage trouble, petty things. His uncle Rafael, ten years Ernesto's senior, lived on La Calma ranch the first fifteen years of Ernesto's life, and little Ernesto would follow his uncle everywhere he went, but Rafael began having problems with the Aviñas and started to leave La Calma for months at a time to find better paying jobs in Texas. From the time he was fifteen, Ernesto had his own pistol, and learned how to shoot, and more importantly how to carry it at all times. The way a modern man won't leave his house without his phone, the macho man wouldn't leave without his pistol. Traditional charro suits, still worn by Mariachi singers, include a side-arm in an ornately tooled leather holster as part of the outfit. Guns are in the cultural makeup of Mexico. I think of such a young person like Ernesto carrying a side holster with him every day, not an uncommon occurrence during his youth, and I ask myself what freedom is, and how we determine its price.

When I had landed at Guadalajara International the day before, I had hired a car service to pick me up at the airport and drive me to the centro. Like I was used to doing in the US, I looked for the designated curbside pickup spot, changing floors between llegadas and salidas, reading signs, frustrated, until I just phoned the driver. *Where are you now?* he asked. I told him I was in an inconvenient spot and could move closer, that I was between a taxi stand and a police officer directing traffic. *Leather jacket? I see you, stay there*, he said and hung up. A car across the divide heading in the wrong direction made an abrupt illegal u-turn and pulled up in front of me, the trunk popping open as it rolled to a halt. I looked at the taxi drivers who would be scowling and cursing at us in the US but ignored us here. Then I looked at the officer who kept directing traffic as if she hadn't seen the maneuver he'd just made in front of her face. I loaded my bag, and when I got in the car I asked him if there was in fact a designated pickup spot. *Nah, it's just wherever you're standing*, the driver told me, *We have real freedom here, not like in the US.*

•

In Tijuana, Juan Limón was finally arrested for the murders sometime in the mid-1950s, and he was sent by plane to serve his time in Guadalajara. He served one year before being released and going back into hiding, knowing Ernesto and the rest of the Vazquez family were still after him. Ernesto implied to me that Juan Limón had some kind of special connection to the prosecutor and was given a sweet deal, though when I pressed him on this detail, his responses became murky and they trailed off. I understood that he didn't want to clarify and so I figured it was best to leave the issue alone. It could have just been a botched trial, shoddy evidence, or lenient sentencing in a country riddled with bullet holes, but there was a vindication in Ernesto's version that I could tell he needed and I was not going to try and take away.

By 1960, Ernesto had entered the police force, and one of his best friends, a taxi driver named Rufino, told him that while driving in San Pedro Tlaquepaque—a town now referred to only as Tlaquepaque, but still called only San Pedro by Ernesto's generation—he had seen Juan Limón selling sugarcane out of a car. Juan Limón was spotted in a town less than ten miles to the east of La Calma, a shorter distance than Manhattan to Queens. Ernesto demanded Rufino tell him where Juan Limón was, but Rufino refused to say anything to Ernesto, fearing something was going to happen that would implicate him.

How much do you want? Because I will pay you to tell me, Ernesto said, *And if you won't do it for the money, then do it for the friendship.*

No way, because you're a real son-of-a-bitch, Ernesto, and if you go and you kill him, then I have to deal with that.

Ernesto assured Rufino that he would never say anything if he were caught, but it did no good, and in the end the friendship suffered great damage for this omission. Refusing to let it go, but now with vague coordinates of Juan Limón's location, a twenty-two-year-old Ernesto was intent on finding him before Limón moved again.

In 1961, Ernesto had a casual conversation with a lieutenant from La Barca—a municipality an hour from Guadalajara, but still in the state of Jalisco—who was fond of him. The lieutenant pointed to Ernesto's limp, and Ernesto told him the story of Juan Limón and that he had been recently spotted in San Pedro.

The lieutenant asked, *Would you recognize him?*

Ernesto nodded and they got into a patrol car, drove directly to Tlaquepaque, and started slowly driving up and down every street in the pueblo. They spent several hours checking and rechecking every place someone could be selling sugarcane out of the trunk of their car. The lieutenant was carrying a sawed off shotgun that he told Ernesto he had used to kill someone already. Some people they had questioned on that route told them they had seen Juan Limón at the large mercado, selling there, so they took the patrol car and parked across the street.

You just tell me which one he is, and don't get down from the car, the lieutenant said, *Don't get this stain on you, I'll do it.*

·

For many years, Ernesto inquired, he searched, he bribed, but he never found Juan Limón. He was chasing a phantom. Later in his life, he heard that Juan Limón ended up in the US, and had soon become diabetic. Not long after that, he was diagnosed with cancer and then came back across the border to Mexicali, just south of Calexico.

My aunt Margarita told me this, Ernesto said, *But it would have been better if she had said nothing.* The bitterness began to rise in his voice. This was a mannerism I was familiar with, mimicked by the other men in our family. Often it was the last emotional signal before rage, but Ernesto took a breath, then continued.

Because if sheeee-, Ernesto emphasized the vowel, and paused, then started again the same way he had left off, *Because if sheeee wanted to, sheee could have told me where he was, because sheee knew, they would visit him, it was her brother.*

Ernesto recognized that Margarita had loyalty to her brother-in-law, but this is where the depth of Mexican family loyalty, beyond reason, beyond ethics, crashed into itself. His aunt may have been aware of what would transpire. She may have been trying to circumvent the violence, save the men from themselves. But the myopic nature of manhood, of the macho man, can be impossible to resist, and Ernesto only showed contempt for his aunt. In his eyes, she chose sides. It was that simple. When Juan Limón's diabetes grew much worse in his old age, he had to have his legs amputated. Ernesto's shoulders slackened when he told me this gruesome detail.

She said he cried like a child to his family, Ernesto said, *And Juan Limón told her, I wish you had told those Vazquezs where I was so they could have just killed me, because I am tired of suffering!*

As Ernesto speaks more about the years spent searching for Juan Limón, I think of the types of inheritance we are left with after lives led in such pain and worry. Sometimes that inheritance is a debt, and like debts that go effortlessly unpaid, it is easy for the lessons to go unlearned; often we arrive too late to their conclusions for them to be of any use to us. My abuelo is gone, his body returned to the Earth leaving only a box of bones, Nene too, yet I am confronted with their ghosts that haunt our family in temporal disjunction. This hauntological accumulation of time breezes through the streets of La Calma, the streets of La Puente, blowing smoke from warm barrels until it joins together in nebulous altitudes, only to fall again and dust those of us left on this Earth until we are indistinguishable from each other.

NC Hernandez is a Chicano writer from southern California, temporarily living in San Francisco since 2010 with his partner and two cats. He has worked as a behaviorist for children with autism, a touring musician, and an immigrant rights activist who led the first visitation program in California for federally imprisoned immigrants. He currently works in a non-profit organization, spends part of the year in Mexico City, and invents his own cocktails. Hernandez writes socio-political essays about male violence, music, and classic menswear.

HORIZONTAL RECRUITERS

by Mark Blickley

A dozen years ago, I visited Arlington National Cemetery for the first (and only) time. As a reluctant participant in the Vietnam War, I was hoping that my visit to this "hallowed ground" would offer up some kind of comfort, some sort of pride, for having served my country during wartime. It provided neither comfort nor pride for me.

I was puzzled by my response. The place is 639 acres of beautifully landscaped graves and monuments. It's situated right on the banks of the Potomac River and offers a majestic view of Washington, D.C. My initial reaction was of awe and a feeling of connection with the names and dates etched on tombstones and mausoleums. But as I explored the cemetery, there were signs strategically placed on pathways admonishing me to keep silent and to be respectful of the dead. At first, I read these signs as a nice way to respect the men and women buried underfoot. Then they annoyed me because of their commanding tone, and finally, they angered me because I felt as if I were back in the service, and some belligerent officer was once again barking out at me how to think and how to behave.

This anger made me feel uncomfortable at Arlington. I thought it was my displaced feelings of resentment at having had to put on a uniform even though I found out after my tour of duty that because of my father's death when I was nine, I needn't have gone into the military at all. Being the only surviving male in a household with my mother and three sisters would have exempted me from service as I was my mother's only source of support. But boys from the Bronx didn't get any kind of anti-war counseling that would illuminate such information—college students and college-bound students had middle-class counselors available to them, not the urban poor. So as I trudged through acre after acre of funereal splendor, I thought my growing repulsion to Arlington was simply a matter of personal "sour grapes," independent of the visual and historical landscape where I had deposited myself.

I was wrong. It suddenly dawned on me that the signs admonishing me to behave in a certain way weren't so much to insure proper respect for the dead, but a kind of recruitment poster for potential future servicemen. In my mind the phrase *eternal rest* suddenly turned into *parade rest*, the military term for being at ease while still in a military formation. I felt that every corpse interred at Arlington was there to seduce living boys to join up and experience the wonders of heroic service to one's country. When I discovered that Arlington National Cemetery was open 365 days a year, from sunrise to sunset, it disturbed me. It seemed as if the dead never had a time to be dead, that they were continually on display, continually in formation to perpetuate a recruiter's dream of power and glory.

Heroic service is the key. Hero. The mythological hero envisioned and praised in ancient literature, where immortality wasn't considered to be taking up residence in an afterlife, but having the deeds of the hero repeated and praised by living generation after generation.

It's not a coincidence that an internationally renowned military cemetery, barely a hundred years old and the national depository of the military dead for a nation not much more than two hundred years old, is architecturally rooted in the ancient past of Greece and Rome where this heroic ideal flourished. It's not America one enters when you pass the gates of Arlington, it's the ancient world of the Theseum in Athens that the cemetery's Greek Revival centerpiece, Arlington House (once the Custis-Lee mansion), imitates. It's that of the white marbled, roofless, memorial amphitheater. "Copied after both the theater of Dionysus at Athens and the Roman theater at Orange, France," according to the *Encyclopedia Britannica*, "the proportions and distances convey the charm of an old Greek ruin."

But this unique American historical monument has become, in addition, a huge recruitment center rooted in the glorious mysteries of ancient legends of death and sacrifice. My feeling that one of the subtler purposes of Arlington National Cemetery is in military recruitment was greatly strengthened when I discovered that the United States government maintains 114 national cemeteries, but Arlington is one of only two under the jurisdiction of the United States Army. The remaining national cemeteries are administered by the Department of Veterans Affairs. Why is Arlington one of only two military cemeteries in the nation administered by an active branch of the military? Does the United States Army, which employs more than ten thousand recruiters that work vertically, see these Arlington dead as important and powerful horizontal recruiters?

In his book, *The Hero with a Thousand Faces*, Joseph Campbell describes the role of ceremonies such as burial:

> *[They] serve to translate the individual's life-crises and life-deeds into classic, impersonal forms. They disclose him to himself, not as this personality or that, but as the warrior.... Generations of individuals pass, like anony-*

mous cells from a living body; but the sustaining, timeless form remains. By an enlargement of vision to embrace this super-individual, each discovers himself enhanced, enriched, supported and magnified.

Campbell is describing the role of burial in the life of ancient, tribal warriors, but is there an Army recruiter in late-20th-century America that wouldn't kill to be able to induce an experience of that magnitude on a daily basis? Arlington National Cemetery does evoke that type of experience every day of the year, from sunrise to sunset. The overwhelming majority of the 230,000 corpses interred there are not heroes, but "ordinary" citizens like the visitors viewing them. But planted within this classically structured cemetery, these acres of ordinary individuals become inspiring "super-individuals" perpetuating the validation of this festival of the dead.

Justice Joseph Story stated in an address at a cemetery dedication in 1831, that contemporary Christian attitudes and practices concerning burial were, unfortunately, not the equal of those of earlier "heathen" cultures, and to prove his point he briefly surveyed the burial customs of the ancient Egyptians, Greeks, Hebrews, and others. "Our cemeteries, rightly selected, and properly arranged, may be made subservient to some of the highest purposes of human duty. They may preach lessons, to which none may refuse to listen, and which all that live must hear."

Participating in this recruitment poetry of the tombs is the most visited site at Arlington, John F. Kennedy's grave. Inscribed on the wall nearby is this quote from his inaugural address: "In the long history of the world, only a few generations have been granted the role of defending freedom in its hour of maximum danger." The irony of such a quote coming from Kennedy is that during World War II, as a naval officer, Lt. John Kennedy was the only P.T. boat commander to lose a boat by enemy ramming in the entire Pacific theater. Through the intervention of his powerful father, Joseph Kennedy, Lt. Kennedy was able to turn his impending court martial for gross neglect of duty into an act of inspirational heroism that propelled him into Congress and eventually into the role of the nation's Commander-in-Chief. John Kennedy now concludes his public career as Arlington's number one military recruiter.

As I delved deeper into the history of Arlington National Cemetery, I was surprised to find that the issue of racial identity is also alive on this hallowed ground. From 1864 until 1890, it served as the site of an encampment for the formerly enslaved known as Freedman's Village. Freedman's Village resulted from Lincoln's emancipation of all enslaved people living in the District of Columbia on April 16, 1862. Given Washington's proximity to the southern states, many escapees from slavery—as well as those liberated by advancing Union troops—found their way there in search of a new life. Overcrowding and disease forced the government to relocate many different camps (including one inside the U.S. Capitol Building) to Arlington as a temporary refuge, but the camp grew to be known as Freedman's Village, providing permanent housing and other community services to liberated Black men, women, and children for nearly thirty years.

At its inception, the village came under the military jurisdiction of the U.S. Army and was governed by a military commander. Many residents complained that life under military rule was not much better than slavery.

After the war, the desire to assist those who had been enslaved lost a great deal of its support among the general public, and fewer and fewer resources were made available to the villagers. Neighboring residents complained of the crime associated with the village and of the financial burden they were forced to assume as federal assistance to the villagers was reduced. By 1890, the villagers were no longer considered refugees from slavery, and Freedman's Village was dismantled and the residents were forced to leave.

Thus, more than three generations before Franklin Roosevelt's administration, a harsh welfare "state" was founded at Arlington National Cemetery. The negative result from this noble experiment proved to be a microcosm of contemporary racial strife. I'm at a loss to explain why this earliest of governmental precedents concerning the race question wasn't factored into 20th-century policy decisions. I imagine that some invaluable insights could be gained by studying how a Freedman's Village, in the course of a single generation, could evolve into what many believe acted as a Freedman's Prison. I suspect that the truth of this failure has been discreetly buried under humanely inscribed Arlington Cemetery monuments, ones that applaud the government's benevolent establishment of Freedman's Village to help the downtrodden African-American victims of the Civil War.

Discreet burials of another kind were performed at Arlington. There existed a policy of segregating Black warriors from white that lasted for nine decades. The expulsion of living Black residents from cemetery grounds in 1890 was replaced with the expulsion of deceased Black residents by depositing their corpses in a separate area, away from their white counterparts. Segregated even in death, Black soldiers were denied the same hero status given to whites. This "Freedman's Village of the Dead" existed until 1948. It's only been seventy years since our Black servicemen and women have been afforded the privilege of serving our nation as horizontal recruiters.

Arlington National Cemetery is a kind of theme-park whose theme is our national, and to a lesser extent, racial identity. Disney World may be the theme-park brainchild of Walt Disney, but Arlington is one of only two national cemeteries out of 114 that is under the direct control of the United States Army, and it's not even the largest national cemetery. It's the theme-park brainchild of the Pentagon that serves a future much more adroitly than the past it claims to represent.

Mark Blickley is a New York based, widely published and produced, author of fiction, nonfiction, drama, poetry, and experimental video, and a proud member of the Dramatists Guild and PEN American Center. His multi-genre collaborations with artist Amy Bassin include *Weathered Reports: Trump Surrogate Quotes from the Underground* (Moira Books) and the text-based art collaboration *Dream Streams* (Clare Songbirds Publishing House). His videos, "Speaking in Bootongue" and "Widow's Peek: The Kiss of Death," represented the United States in the 2020 year-long international world tour of Time Is Love: Universal Feelings: Myths & Conjunctions, organized by esteemed Togolese-French curator, Kisito Assangni.

THE SUITCASE

by Heather Diamond

Amah is in the kitchen, and I hear her scolding Abah in Cantonese before he comes back with the suitcase and sets it on the coffee table. A little larger than a briefcase, it's made of heavy cardboard lacquered a faded reddish brown and has a brass sliding lock, corner caps, and hinged handles. The sides are scuffed. When he opens it, we see that it is lined with yellowed newspaper covered in Chinese characters. Eager to empty the case, Abah begins lifting out papers and old photographs that he piles to one side.

Fred lets out an exasperated sigh and says to me, "He wants me to have it because it belonged to my grandma. I told him we don't have room, but he won't listen. He never does. You just have to humor him."

We've been in Hong Kong two weeks now, and we've already outgrown our luggage. I glance nervously at Abah to see if he overheard. I've noticed he follows our conversations in English, smiling and nodding on occasion, but I never know how much he understands because he's too shy to speak it.

Fred sifts through the pile, showing me pictures of his family. *Here's my mom when she was young. This is their wedding picture. Here's my grandma.* He stops short at a black and white photo of Abah as a young man standing in front of a painted studio backdrop. He's wearing the drab hat and quilted jacket of Mao's communist army—his baggy pants and jacket too large for his slight frame, his right hand resting on the holster of a gun strapped to his leather belt. His slender, unsmiling face with the large ears is the face of a pensive dreamer, not a soldier.

"What's this?" Fred dangles the photo in front of his father, who chuckles with his hand over his mouth. "I've never seen this one before!" Fred says to me. Abah picks up another photo that shows a group of young soldiers and points to himself in the back row, the same unsmiling expression amidst a group of boys in soldier outfits.

Abah points and identifies a man in the front row. "His friend who helped him escape," Fred says. As his father's storytelling picks up speed, I am caught in the lag-time before translation. Primed for suspense, drama, and comedy before I know the story. Abah is agitated as he continues:

I was young and idealistic. I ran after the communists' truck and told them I wanted to join up. At first, they didn't believe me. They said I looked like a weak city boy, but I said I wanted to teach the peasants to read, to be one of the send-down youth, so they finally took me.

"He says his superior trusted him with a leadership position and a gun," Fred says, "but he never wanted to have a gun or be in charge. He wanted out." Abah resumes the story as soon as Fred stops:

I didn't trust anyone, but there was one guy who never got anything from home, so I shared my packages from home with him and loaned him money. Then your grandma wrote me a letter saying she was sick. I decided to trust this guy and found out he wanted to leave too. So we came up with a plan to escape together.

As Abah's story unfolds, I picture it all in black and white, like an old newsreel. Beneath it another reel, one I have often tried and failed to conjure, remains hazy and full of questions.

My grandfather and his siblings migrating to America to escape the pogroms in Ukraine. My grandmother's family dispersing as a result of the Russian Revolution. In each of these, the backdrop goes up in smoke.

Abah waits for Fred to finish, then leans forward as he continues:

At the end of our training, there was a banquet to celebrate our graduation. During the banquet, the other guy and I stood up and announced that there wasn't enough food and we were going out for more. As soon as we were out of the banquet hall, we changed out of our uniforms into street clothes and ran for the train platform.

Abah is standing now, eyes wide and arms waving. Then he crouches down and mimes a hobbling, bent-over run, bobbing up several times to look over his shoulder. I've never seen him this animated.

When we didn't come back, guards were sent to find us. We could see them coming, so we ducked behind an old woman carrying heavy bags on a cart and barely made it to the train by hiding behind her. I had to hide out in Hong Kong for a while after I got home because they were still looking for me. They came to the house, but your grandma always said she didn't know where I was.

Abah sits quietly, his hands resting on his pajama-covered knees. He watches my face while Fred translates. "Wow," Fred says, leaning back and shaking his head. "I never knew he was a communist!" My astonishment at Abah's story is tinged with sadness and envy. I wish I could open my own grandmother's suitcase and unpack my family history.

Amah has wandered in from the kitchen, and now she points her finger at Abah and teases in a tone I once thought accusatory. The men laugh, and Fred explains, "Mom says they were on opposite sides because her father was a high-ranking general in the Kuomintang. She could have married a general, but instead she ended up with this communist sympathizer."

Fred snaps pictures of the photos before Abah stacks them into a box. Then he latches the empty suitcase that now belongs to him.

Heather Diamond is an American writer in Hong Kong. She earned a Ph.D. in American Studies from the University of Hawaii and has worked as a bookseller, university lecturer, and museum curator. She is the author of *Rabbit in Moon: a Memoir* and *American Aloha: Cultural Tourism and the Negotiation of Tradition.* Her essays have appeared in *(Her)oics: Women's Lived Experiences of the Pandemic, Memoir Magazine, Sky Island Journal, Rappahannock Review, Waterwheel Review, Hong Kong Review,* and *New South Journal.*

PHOTOGRAPHS AND MEMORIES

by Geoff Hart

It begins innocently enough with what I jokingly refer to as "senior brain." I find I can't remember the name of someone I'm thinking of, even if I can clearly see their face. At first, it's just actors. Later, it becomes acquaintances. Five minutes after the conversation has moved on, I remember—it's the *esprit de l'escalier* from Hell. Early on, I just shake my head ruefully and move on. Later, I often slap my forehead and speak the name, completely out of context. It confuses people, so I teach myself to stop doing that.

Things progress. One day, I can't find my eyeglasses because I've forgotten that I pushed them up on my forehead. Another day, I pour boiling water on the teabag and two hours later, stumble across the stone-cold cup of tea I've forgotten. But it gets worse. Like the night I find myself staring at the remote for what seems like an hour, trying and failing to figure out how to turn on the TV, only to discover I'm holding the remote for the satellite dish. In fairness, I've got six remotes sitting on the coffee table before the TV, and three of them have the same brand name, making it nearly impossible to tell which one goes with which device. Trial and error would be easier if I remembered which ones I'd already tried, or remembered to replace the batteries so the correct remote for a task, when I eventually find it, actually does what I want it to do.

I resolve to label each remote with masking tape once I figure out what it does. I forget to do this. Again.

It could just be senior brain, or…

"I won't sugarcoat this, Dan. It's almost certainly early-onset dementia. Probably some form of Alzheimer's given your family history. We'll need to do some imaging studies to be sure. But given your descriptions and your family history, that's my best guess."

We book an appointment in a month for a bunch of TLAs—three letter acronyms, I remember—and he pats me on the shoulder. "We'll see you in a month, Dan. In the meantime, if your wife can't drive you, maybe leave your car at home and take public transit. And you and your wife are going to need counselling to get you through this. It won't be easy." He gives me a sheet of paper with the names and contact info for some therapists.

I nod, and I'm halfway home before I remember my wife left me a year ago for reasons I can't remember, and I somehow neglected to mention it to my doctor. I pull over, and let the tears spill down my cheeks. Sorrow turns to fear, fear turns to anger—and I park my car somewhere safe, figuring I'm in no condition to drive. I hope I'll remember where I left it.

I remember my imaging appointment—or, to be fair, Siri remembers it for me. I lie, motionless and with head restrained, for what seems like a day in the MRI machine, a claustrophobic and inauspiciously coffin-like structure, staccato sounds of the device's powerful magnets like someone knocking on a tin roof with a triphammer.

Or throwing dirt on the lid of my coffin.

When it's over, they pull me out into the world again, and I squint against the brightness of the overhead light. I can't remember where I've left my clothing, but a kind nurse brings me to the lockers. Only I can't remember the lock's combination. Drama ensues while we discover they don't have it written down anywhere, and we have to wait for one of the maintenance staff to cut the lock with a giant pair of bolt cutters. Turns out I left the paper containing the combination inside the locker.

In the doctor's office, the doctor is frowning. "I'm sorry Dan, it's variant 3-alpha Alzheimer's." I'm numb, having expected this but not really grasped it emotionally. I can't tell you how many times I've hit the Mayo Clinic website to consult the list of symptoms. No, I *literally* can't tell you how often. The sense of déjà vu tells me it's been many times, but I simply can't remember.

"Beg pardon?"

I've drifted away, and the doctor's sudden silence tells me that.

"I was saying, Dan, that we don't really have any treatment for the cognitive decline. There are some promising genetic therapies that attack a few genes that we *think* are responsible for the decline. But they're in clinical trials, and I don't think you'll qualify. Also, I've got to be honest with you, the early results aren't all that promising. It's a complicated disease."

Fear surges, but I manage to master it before it becomes anger. I've had lots of practice. "In my place, what would you do?"

He sits back in his chair, and I can see the bleak look in his eyes. Probably thinking, *throw myself off the nearest tall building*. I know that's where I'm going with this. But instead he gets hold of himself and sits up straighter.

"We can't cure it, but we can help you manage the symptoms. There's an interesting trial going on at the university that uses augmented reality to help people with dementia manage their environment better."

"Augmented reality… you mean like Google Glass?"

"Yes, only better."

"What you're saying is, when you look at me, you think *glasshole*." I laugh at my own joke; he smiles dutifully. He may be *thinking* that, but he's too much the pro to actually admit it.

"If you'd like, I can call them and see if they need any testers."

"Please do that. And thanks."

"I'll also put you on the waitlist for a social worker. You're going to need to transition to a long-term care facility sooner rather than later." He sighs. "I'm sorry I can't do more for you. We like to think the white coats make us angels, but modern medicine is in many ways still a black art."

We shake hands, I leave the office, and when I reach the street, it takes a moment to orient myself. Where did I leave my God-damned car this time? I let the fear become anger—at myself, at the world, at God. The anger helps me focus, and I recall that I left the car at home, not feeling safe driving it any longer. It takes a bit longer to remember which bus I need to take to get home. I don't remember anything about the trip, but I must have asked the driver to announce my stop, since he yells at me and, intimidated, I hunch my shoulders like he's going to hit me and exit through the rear door.

I forget my appointment at the university, but they haven't forgotten me. They apparently have a good grasp of the kind of person they're working with, and call me an hour before to remind me of the appointment, tell me they're sending a grad student with a car to pick me up, and call me again when she's getting closer so that I remember to come downstairs. She's a young Asian woman who introduces herself, holds the door open for me, helps me with my seatbelt, and doesn't seem to resent me when I ask her for her name again. Twice.

At the lab, I meet Doctor Roberts. (I remember his name not because he repeats it, but because he has a name tag clipped to his shirt pocket. Apparently my visual memory is still intact, even if the rest of my memory has left the building when I wasn't looking.) He's Black and looks familiar, somehow.

"Dan, I'll be your neurologist from here on. I'd like to introduce you to the rest of the crew." He repeats the Asian woman's name, but it goes in one ear and out the other, just like the names of their hardware engineer, software engineer, and artificial-intelligence specialist. Sadly, I guess they're not self-important enough for name tags, and I can't see their security badges without squinting inappropriately.

"So let me start by asking: do you know what augmented reality is?"

I mumble a halfhearted description, but do remember the term *glasshole*. They exchange glances, but nobody laughs.

Roberts continues. "That's basically right, Dan. The idea's to provide you with an assistive device that will figure out what you're looking at using artificial intelligence. For someone who's not facing the challenges you're facing, we have a cell phone app—you just point a smartphone camera at an object and the phone tells you what it is. But Alzheimer's patients often lose the ability to remember how the phone works. For them, we recommend a pair of glasses. You already wear glasses, so the adaptation shouldn't be too difficult."

The engineer whose name I still can't remember opens a box that's been sitting on the lab bench beside him, and removes a pair of surprisingly stylish eyeglasses. The left earpiece has a thin trailing cable that connects to a blocky black-plastic case about the size of a cell phone. A battery, presumably. Maybe a portable hard drive. There's a faint flicker of light coming from each temple of the glasses.

"Want to take it for a spin?"

A former president. That's who the doctor looks like. Now if only I could remember the guy's name.

Not important.

I nod, and engineer boy places the battery or whatever in my shirt pocket, gently removes my glasses, then pushes back my hair and loops the earpieces over my ears. Through the glasses, I see a translucent rectangle floating above the object nearest the center of my visual field. When I pan my head, the rectangle jumps to other objects. It's disorienting at first, but my eyes quickly adjust to the motion. When I return my gaze to the man who's been talking, and focus on his face, two icons appear: the outline of a mouth and the outline of a page filled with text. I focus on the page icon, and the words "Doctor Roberts, MD" appear above his face. When I focus on the name, his LinkedIn page appears, blocking his face until I glance away from it and it fades. I look at his face again, and this time focus on the mouth icon. In my ears, I hear the words "Doctor Alan Roberts." I tap my ear, reaching for an earbud.

"Bone conduction," says engineer boy. "That way, there's no need for dedicated earphones. They're just too easy to lose. And they break. But there's a speaker in the battery pack in case you misplace the glasses." I look at him. *Ramirez*, the glasses say.

I feel a grin spreading across my face. "That's so damned cool!"

Grins from the whole team. Roberts nods. "We're pretty pleased with it. There are still some glitches, of course, but we can upgrade the software wirelessly as we spot the problems and fix them. So the performance should improve incrementally. That's what"—he says a name that I immediately forget—"will be doing with the AI: teaching it to recognize not just the identity of an object, but also its significance to you. We'll work with you to ensure the software learns your needs and prioritizes those contexts accordingly."

The AI person speaks. I can't tell whether they're a he, a she, or a they, and don't know whether that's normal or just another mental lapse on my part. "The software will have to monitor you 24/7. So we need you to sign a waiver to permit that monitoring. It's a bit of an invasion of privacy..." I look at them, and the glasses display *Rashad*, which doesn't help.

I shrug. "It's not like I'll have any illusion of privacy once I'm in the residence."

"There's a modesty feature. Click the icon at the top of the screen... the one with the smiley face holding hands over its eyes. There you go!"

"You think I'm going to remember that?"

Rashad laughs. "The software will recognize a toilet or shower stall and make the icon flash to remind you it's there. Before you ask: it'll reset when you leave the room, so you can't forget and leave it turned off."

Roberts hands me a multi-page paper contract, not meeting my eyes, and I sign it without reading it. "Date please?" Roberts supplies the date, and I write it beside my signature. He takes the paper and pen from me, countersigns, and hands it to the Asian girl. *Tran*, say the glasses.

"Great! We'll leave you with Doctor Rashad to learn and customize the interface. You've figured out how to choose text versus speech. They'll run you through the calibration routines and settings."

They leave, and Rashad and I spend a few hours playing with the technology. Then they confiscate the glasses and promise to deliver them the next day, with the necessary tweaks. When I return home, I find the kettle's boiled dry.

Fortunately, unlike the stove that's also on, it has an automatic shutoff.

Engineer boy—Ramirez—comes the next day with the glasses, and we encounter our first problem: I can't remember the password for Siri, so he can't pair the glasses with my network. That doesn't stop him; he picks up the smart speaker, pulls the plug, then reboots it, tinkering with something I can't see. That quickly, the glasses are online, and when I look at the speaker, the password appears. I'm tempted to Google him and learn who I'm dealing with, but decide it's not worth it. I'm just going to forget him again.

He walks me around the apartment, iPad in hand, examining a long checklist of objects: light switches, appliances, remote controls, bathroom amenities... pretty much everything I interact with on a daily basis. For each one, he interrogates me to learn how I use it, and as I explain, he taps a bunch of settings. It takes a couple hours, but by the end of it, anything I look at has its own tag and my medication schedule has been recorded somewhere along the way, since the glasses remind me it's time for my afternoon pills. To test the glasses, I try turning on the oven. When I do, a red icon appears, blinking at the top of my left lens. When I stare at it, a popup appears: *The oven is on. Please turn it off when you're done.*

Impressive!

Before engineer boy leaves, he reminds me to plug in the battery each night for recharging. "The glasses will remind you," he adds, "but you'll feel more in control if you can do this yourself."

As the door closes, I remember the oven. Well, the blinking indicator reminds me to turn it off. So I do before I forget, and the indicator vanishes. I putter in the kitchen, making a simple omelet, with only a little bit of shell in it. The glasses display a reminder of the steps required, and a reminder to turn off the burner when I'm done. I'm pissed off at it, since I still remember how to cook an omelet, but the anger passes when I turn on the television on the first try. I've got to admit, it's nice having an assistant who knows the technology far better than I ever will. That night, as I sit on my bed, a reminder chimes in my ear: *Recharge your battery*. I plug it in, wondering how I'm ever going to remember the glasses in the morning.

But they've thought of that too. The battery has a motion sensor and speaker. When I rise at 2 AM to take a piss, as I do every night, it reminds me to put on the glasses. I do, and ignore the humiliating pop-up that reminds me to flush when I'm done and jiggle the handle to ensure that the water won't keep running all night.

I carry on with my normal routine, interrupted only by an occasional phone call from the researchers. *Do I need help with X*, and *is Y functioning the way I want it to function*? Yes, yes, everything's great. Now leave me alone! But it really is great. I feel enormously safer, and I'm not feeling the frustration that leads to those unpredictable rages that often end with me wiping hot tears from my cheeks, wishing I could just let loose and break something.

The days pass, and a social worker arrives to talk with me. She's a tiny Latina with fierce eyes and a no-nonsense way of working through her checklist. She's obviously coordinated with the university team, since she knows about the glasses and can download my activity logs direct to her iPad. Before I can decide I'd like to remember her name, she's done and out the door. I spend a few minutes trying, unsuccessfully, to figure out how to learn her name. About the time I'm ready to give up, I notice the business card she's left on my coffee table. Maria Hernández, Master's in Social Work, BA in senior psychology. She's cute, and has an amazing smile. I stare at the business card until a dialog box appears. I click OK so the glasses will remember her name and pair it with an image.

Time passes, and the long-term care facility sends people to help me pack. I'll be moving from my current apartment, with two bedrooms, into a single room, which means I'm going to have to downsize radically. The thought makes me extremely sad, and I turn away from the packers to hide my tears. This time, the Asian woman's here to help. *Tran*, say the glasses, as she tinkers with her iPad and updates the software. Gopinder, the big Sikh orderly, pats my shoulder and offers me a hug that I reject. But not in an unkind way. And I find myself wondering how in Hell I've remembered his name, until I notice the large-print name badge on his shirt. I sigh.

The only good thing about dementia is that once I've sorted my possessions into keep and discard piles, I promptly forget the discards, unless my gaze happens to wander across them. Those few times I recall what I'm missing, the glasses remind me that I've discarded it. Another nice thing about the glasses is that they're infinitely patient. They don't get frustrated when I ask them the same question twenty times. Or thirty, or…

I don't remember anything about my move to the long-term care facility. Just a sense of sadness at what I've left behind, even if I can't evoke exactly what it is that's making me sad. My new home is a small but comfortable room. The bed is smaller, as it's a single bed, and the room's equipped with a variety of gadgets that start out bewildering, until I focus on them and explanations appear. At the end of my first day, I go to the welcome desk to ask when I'll be returning home. Gopinder smiles sadly and covers my hand with his. "Dan, *this* is your home now." Gopinder turns out to have the patience of a saint, since I ask him the same question every day for the next week. But by the end of that week, he's clearly had words with the university people; when I put on my coat and head for the welcome desk, my glasses flash an alert: *You're already home, Dan.* Oh. That's reassuring. Engineer boy visits to hook me up to the network. Hernández? *No*, the glasses correct me: *Ramirez.* I find myself missing Doctor Ex-president and the Asian girl. *Tran.* There's a fourth person I can't remember, and whom I'm not motivated to look up.

There's one woman who lies in bed all day, moaning. Periodically, she screams for help. The other residents, who seem mostly nice, have learned to ignore her but I can't do it. It's nails-on-a-chalkboard horrible, and the only reprieve comes at night, when they sedate her. One day, inspiration strikes, and I ask my glasses whether anything can be done about the sound. Something *can* be done: it turns out the earpieces can do that noise-cancellation trick. It doesn't completely eliminate her cries, but reduces them to a tolerable mosquito buzz at the edge of perception.

One day, another inspiration strikes. Sure, this is my new home, but there's a door. It's not guarded for long stretches, since there are security measures to keep us inmates from leaving. But I find that it's not hard to linger within sight of the keypad that visitors and staff use to leave. My glasses record the codes, and the next time there's a shift change, with all the orderlies and medical staff meeting in the break room, I grab my coat and make a run for it. Everything's going great until I get the door open and run smack into Gopinder's broad chest. The subway ran late, so he's 15 minutes late for work today.

"Where you going, Dan?" He places a gentle, but very strong, hand on my shoulder, turns me around, and holds the door for me.

I'm going nowhere, clearly. Damn. Maybe the glasses can do a better job of watching for openings tomorrow? But tomorrow, the keypad code is changed, and when I ask the glasses to record the new one, they refuse. Damn twice. Guess Gopinder had a few words with the researchers.

We settle into a routine. I get to know the people I share my space with, and like I said, they're mostly nice. I spend a lot of time playing cards or checkers or backgammon. Anything, really, that involves social interaction. Anything except chess and strategy games—I find it too hard to look ahead several moves and remember what I saw. The other games rapidly become boring until I regretfully instruct the glasses to stop helping me with my play. Once I stop winning most games, my interest revives. We share our opinions on the news of the day but mostly ignore politics. That's a very different world, and one we don't belong to anymore. Those of us who've been warehoused don't get to vote anymore, for instance. I'm not sure whether that's policy, or just benign neglect.

Most of my ward-mates have brought photographs of loved ones: deceased wives, children, grandchildren. I recall having a wife, and can almost bring her face to mind, but I don't have any photos to share. My parents have been dead for years, and I never had children. The glasses tell me I don't have any close relatives either. One man gets upset when I tell him I have no photos. He doesn't believe me, and thinks I'm holding out on him. Finally, I get fed up and order a couple picture frames, print some photos I find on my glasses, and have them delivered. I install them on my dresser, where anyone who visits can see them. Now that I'm sharing, we become fast friends and spend a lot of time playing gin rummy. He never asks why my son is Black and looks like a former president, or why my daughter's Vietnamese. Good thing. I don't know the answer. Adopted, maybe?

One day, I notice a short blond child with a dark brown face standing in a corner, watching me. I call out to her, but she keeps staring. I focus the glasses on her, and the word *sunflower* appears over her head. Strange name for a girl, but I've heard stranger. I think. I can't remember for sure. So I shout her name louder, thinking maybe she's hard of hearing. She continues to ignore me. I get irate, enough so that Gopinder comes running to see what the trouble is.

"There's no one there, Dan." He pats my shoulder soothingly.

"Don't be a fool, Gopinder. I see her, clear as day. Right there. In the corner."

Gopinder sighs and goes over to fetch her. He gently takes my hand and places it on the girl's hair. And it turns out not to be a girl at all, but rather a flower. A *sunflower*. I'm so ashamed my cheeks heat up and I'm about ready to start crying. Gopinder pats my shoulder again. "It's probably your meds. I'll ask the doctors to up the dose of your antipsychotic."

I'm taking meds? The glasses confirm it.

In the coming days, the blond girl keeps returning to watch me, but I'm less agitated about it than I used to be. She wants to be antisocial? Fine. Her loss. Everyone else here *loves* me.

We don't have much use for money at the residence. Everything's pretty much paid for, done by automated monthly withdrawals from my account. That works fine until the cheque bounces, so to speak. There's something wrong with my bank account. There should be more money. I rummage through my desk until I turn up my cheque book. Yes, I know, using a cheque book is so 20th century. But it's not like I have a choice. I can't remember how to use my damned online banking, even though the password manager in my glasses lets me log in. The residence manager calls Roberts and his crew, and lo and behold, it turns out the glasses have been recording me night and day in the interest of improving the software. I don't recall giving them permission to do that, but I must have done so and forgotten. They seem like nice people, not the kind who'd do something like that if I hadn't told them it was okay.

Anyway, it turns out one of the orderlies was using the glasses while I slept. He found the password manager app and cracked the main password. Turns out choosing an obvious password (Daniel) isn't so clever as I thought. Hackers don't follow the common logic of "nobody would be stupid enough to use such an obvious password." While the cops are frog-marching the orderly out the door, a fellow who looks vaguely familiar—*Rashad*, say the glasses—replaces my glasses with a new model that can recognize some pattern in my eyes as a password. No worry that anyone's going to hack *my* glasses again.

One day, I receive a visit from the former president of the United States. Why he's visiting me, I have no idea. My glasses tell me *Doctor Roberts*, but they're clearly buggy. I know who it is visiting me. He looks sad, but that's not unusual. Most of the people who visit us look sad.

"The thing is," he says, not meeting my eyes, "we've run into money problems. This kind of cutting-edge research is pricey, and the university's under severe financial pressure these days. So they brought in a bunch of venture capitalists who are willing to fund promising projects like ours. Which is great, but it means we're no longer in control of our own research. The first thing they did was fire Abdel." *Doctor Rashad*, the glasses tell me. "They've brought in their own programmer. Dan, I can't tell you how sorry I am about this. I'll do my best to fight for you, but… hell. You understand how it is, right?"

Yeah, I understand. Nobody bears the weight of the world quite like the President. It's why they all go grey so young. I shake his hand, ask him to sign his photo. An odd look crosses his face, but he takes the marker I give him and scrawls something across an empty corner. The signature doesn't look right, but I'm not going to tell him how to sign his own name. As he leaves, he wishes me well, and there's a profound sadness in his eyes.

It's a rough week. My hands start trembling, and sometimes they won't obey me, or obey with a time lag, like a stutter but for the muscles. When I complain, Gopinder tells me they've changed one of my meds. Doctor's orders. I ask for the name, which of course flies in one ear and out the other, but the glasses remember. It's a new antipsychotic, and Google tells me it can apparently cause symptoms similar to those of Parkinson's disease. But it's supposed to be safe for seniors, and it's very profitable for the company that developed it since there aren't any generic alternatives. I shrug. Pharmacists have to earn a living too, right? But I liked the old meds better—I didn't knock my coffee on the floor half the time when I reached for it. My glasses are no help. They show me the optimal path to the cup, but if my muscles won't obey me, that's no damned help. I almost throw them away—then I reconsider. I do decide to leave them on my night stand before breakfast the next day, despite their entreaties to come back for them. But not understanding anything that's going on around me is, bluntly, terrifying. Next day, they're back on again. I ask if I can have my old meds back. Gopinder asks the doctor who prescribed them, and tells me they're not willing. His big brown eyes are sad, and he places a gentle hand on my shoulder.

I'm mostly accustomed to the tremors now, despite having to use a walker to get around without falling, but now I'm having a hard time thinking straight. I ask my glasses, and it turns out that's another side-effect of the new meds. I ask again to change back to the old meds, and they refuse again. But a stranger shows up the next day, an offensively cheerful young white man who fiddles with something on my glasses. When he places the ear pieces behind my ears again, there's a new icon.

"Click the icon," he says, "and you can browse the web from your glasses. It'll help stave off that cognitive decline you're experiencing. Get that old grey matter thinking again!" He pats my shoulder. I shrug off his hand, annoyed. "Try it! There's a content filter to protect you from anything harmful."

I already know how to browse the web, but maybe content filtering is a good idea. So I click the icon, and the lenses fill with a welcome message and a link that points to a company web page. I click it. It's for a pharmaceutical company with a vaguely familiar name. They have a special offer for wearers of my glasses: a reduced price for stocks in the company.

"You said it protects me from harm?"

"You have my word on it."

I give the glasses permission to access my bank account.

Author's notes: For a story that focuses on memory loss, the only possible choice of tense was the present. Dedicated to the memory (no pun intended) of my father.

Geoff Hart (he/him) works as a scientific editor, specializing in helping scientists who have English as their second language publish their research. He also writes fiction in his spare time and has sold 38 stories thus far. Visit him online at www.geoff-hart.com.

FICTION

AN ORAL AND DOCUMENTARY HISTORY OF MY GREAT-AUNT LISSA WILDER

by Joanna Michal Hoyt

What James Proctor Said To Me

You're Lissa Wilder's great-niece, hmmm? Did you know her well? No? But she left you her place anyway. Maybe nobody really did know Lissa Wilder well—nobody but the one man, and we never met him.

No, I don't know who he was—I never saw him with her, but it doesn't take a rocket scientist to figure out what a woman goes to do in the middle of a full-moon night, slipping through the woods without a light, or what a woman comes back from just a little before sunrise, with her hair all mussed up, singing the sweetest little tune.

I wasn't being a nosey-parker. I heard my chickens carrying on, and I thought it was the raccoon after them again, so I came out, and then I saw this light going by all furtive-like, just over the stone wall on her side. I thought maybe it was a burglar, so I went up quiet, with no light, and then I saw it was her. I told myself it wasn't my business what she was up to, but then I thought if something happened to her, if she got hurt, and I'd slunk off and not stayed by to help her…and then I called myself a Peeping Tom and some worse names. I couldn't make myself follow her and I couldn't make myself go back inside, so I was still there before sunrise when she came back, singing, never noticing me.

Loved her? I daresay I did.

What Gillian Randall Said To Me

Your great-aunt Lissa was the best thing that ever happened to me. I didn't mind that they said she was crazy. During the day, I helped her weed that big old garden, and she sent strawberries and squash home with me and never mocked me for finding the bugs more interesting than creepy. By night—

I was trespassing in her woods the first time. We had a yard with a pocket of lawn and no woods, and the moon was high and full, and I didn't know I was a witch then—I thought I might just be crazy, but I knew I wanted to be alone with the moon and the trees. So I slipped down the road and across her hayfield and into the woods. She was in the clearing with the silver birches, dancing and singing a wild tune I'd never heard. I thought, who cares if she's crazy? Look at her! I saw her there other nights, always in the same place, until the night that poor, gossiping fool Velma Marks followed me. After that, I did feel like a trespasser, and I didn't go back. I think Velma did. She used to sigh and shake her head about Lissa like she knew something dreadful. She's got no use for witches, our Velma. It's mutual.

What Velma Marks Said To Me

Why are you asking me about old Miss Wilder? I never told on her. I swear, I never.

I guess you're right, it can't hurt her now, and someone ought to bury it in the right place, where they can say the right words over it. She said something when she buried it, but I couldn't hear what.

No, I just saw the box. But it was just the right size for a baby, and why else should she sneak out into the woods to bury it, and then cry and whisper to it?

Yes...yes, I'll show you where. If there's a ghost haunting the place, it'll be glad we came for it. But we mustn't go at night!

What I Heard Velma Telling Gillian, Who Caught My Eye Over Velma's Shoulder But Managed To Keep A Straight Face

We went out in the woods where I saw that crazy Miss Wilder...well, not to put too fine a point on it, and I might as well tell you since I've already told that bony girl from away who's gotten her place, and what she expects to do with it is more than I know...where I saw her bury her baby. I took that girl there, and I won't deny my knees were knocking when she dug up the box—shallow, too shallow, I thought—and then all that was in it was a few sheets of paper folded up, with Miss Wilder's spikety writing on them. Maybe a confession, maybe she buried the baby somewhere else. Or else... Now, of course, I don't set any store by talk of witchcraft, but ... That girl wouldn't let me read it.

What I Found Written On The Papers In My Great-Aunt's Box

This is the fourth time I've buried this box. I hope it will be the last.

First I buried it with George's letters inside. I should have burned them before I bought the farm and moved out here. Instead I brought them with me and buried them after a year; cried a little, felt lighter afterward and came back singing, and then realized James Proctor was watching me over the wall. I didn't want to explain, so I pretended I hadn't noticed James, but I felt him watching me later—not with the pitying look people had given the old maid with her muddy clothes and loud goats, but with a frightened reverent look that pleased me and set me to thinking on my story as he might have seen it.

I spent five years writing the novel that story grew into, three years sending it away and getting the manuscript back. After the forty-ninth rejection, I actually read it again, cover to cover, as a stranger might, and I saw why they rejected it. So I took it on out to the woods. I dug up the box I'd used to bury George's letters—an old cartridge box my uncle gave me; he said it would keep anything in the ground in good shape—and found the letters still readable. I shoved them back in the ground unprotected, and I wedged my manuscript into that box and buried it again. Again I felt a weight come off me. This time I did my singing way back in my own woods where it wouldn't upset James Proctor. I sang a little tune that came into my head just then, and I looked up at the moon and started to dance a little dance that went with the tune. I turned to go home, and I saw a shadow slipping through the trees. When it went through a shaft of light I saw it was Gillian Randall who used to help me in the garden. A smart girl, that one, and lonely, but I thought that night she wanted to be alone. Still, after that she looked at me as though I was something a sight more exciting than she had expected, and I liked that.

I began to think on what else might interest her and keep her coming back to me. I suppose I was lonely too. I collected things—from the woods, from the box of souvenirs I brought back from my summer with George at the ocean, from the little thrift stores—that I thought would serve as buried treasure for an imaginative girl. I spent most of a year collecting, and then on a full-moon night I went out to the clearing and dug up the box again. It wasn't quite the right sort of box for buried treasure, but it would have to do. I went slowly, and made sure by the sounds that Gillian was following me. She was a little closer and clumsier than usual, I thought. I went out and dug the box up, shoved the manuscript in the bare ground where it belonged (George's letters had disintegrated already), poured the treasures in from a bag under my coat, keeping my back to the noises, and glanced back over my shoulder to be sure Gillian could see what I was doing.

I saw poor addled Velma Marks staring at me, quivering a little, looking—excited? Horrified? I didn't know. I looked at her, at that strange, lonely woman making her life up out of other people's stories, and saw myself in a mirror I didn't like. I was crying as I buried the box again, muttering to myself, "You fool. You fool!"

The next week, I came around a shelf at the library and almost walked into Velma. She stared at me and actually ran away. I started wondering what she thought I had done—what she thought I had buried. I couldn't quite think how to ask, or explain, and after that she avoided me like the plague, so I never could—never had to. But she stayed on my mind, so I wrote this explanation and decided to put it in the box and bury it back in the woods in case she ever comes investigating.

I hope these pages are the last thing I'll have to bury. I hope I can live my own story in the light and find it enough. I don't know. I don't know.

Joanna Michal Hoyt lives with her family on a Catholic Worker farm in rural northern New York, USA, where she spends her days tending goats, gardens, and guests and her evenings reading and writing odd stories. Her short fiction has appeared in publications including *Mysterion*, *On Spec*, and *After Dinner Conversation*. Propertius Press will publish her historical novel *Cracked Reflections* in summer 2021. Read more at https://joannamichalhoyt.com.

BEAUTIFUL MOUNTAIN

by Stephen O'Donnell

Bedsore and thirsty, she lay for days in the darkness. Curled upon a soiled rubber mattress. She knew it must be close to noon. By the heat. By the smell. She knew too that the roaring would begin soon.

You cannot stop your ears against the horrors of this world.

Down the hall, the old man began to wail.

Water, he called. Water. God almighty is there no water to be had? I can't get out of this bed. Someone? Water?

She never recognised the voice. Hungry, weak, and half mad, he called and called amid the noonday stench. Death and shit and the unanswered cries of a thirsty man.

How many more days does the bastard have? Who counted out his allotment, pared the others of theirs? Christ almighty, doesn't he see the futility in it yet? He must by now. He must. He must. She strained to listen until all she could hear was her own blood, burning in her ears.

The old man cried out a final time and then the only sound in the darkness was the drone of bluebottles over the dead.

•

They never shut out the lights. Rora? The old woman sat up slightly in the bed. They ought to've turned out the lights. Shouldn't they?

Aurora looked at the face of the other woman in the bed. Maybe it's an electrical problem.

No. Rora? She shook her hand. No. That has never, they should've, on their rounds, they should've turned them out. This morning. And now look, the sun is well up. Look.

In the street outside, a car alarm rang and rang, unanswered.

Well, don't go getting agitated about it.

Agitated? Rora, really? Do you know how much my son pays them? Don't talk to me about agitation. They should've come around once already today. Shouldn't they? Rora? Are you listening? What about my sugars?

Aurora waved her hand past her ear. I hear you. The whole corridor can hear you.

What's gotten into you?

Aurora shifted in the chair. Amor, they're not, she said. Well, Suzi, they're gone.

What? Be serious. Gone? Where to? And how could you know that? Rora? Hmm? How? Tell me.

Aurora watched her. I don't know, she said and she smiled. *Since she looked out the window. At the parking lot, empty the last three days. At the birds that hopped and dotted undisturbed for over an hour across the motorway lanes.* Let me find you some chocolate.

•

Watching the telenews in the dayroom. Numb to the projected maps and the daily toll of the dead. Nobody listened. Change the channel. Measles spreading, rampant across the Northern Ubangi territory. Six thousand dead.

Change it again. Misery beyond reckoning condensed into a blue television signal.

The days went on.

It had been too distant to mention and now it was so close as to not bear contemplating.

Aurora turned away, gazed through the French doors at the midday sun. Something moved in the shade beneath the trees. She lifted her spectacles from her stomach. On the edge of the lawns, near the schoolyard fence, a heron put out its narrow bill, something small and wriggling, speared upon the tip. She blinked and the bird was gone.

They spoke about it in the television room amid the dusty blinds and the advertisers' drone like something occurring at a vast distance. A stellar display of no consequence. Someone changed the channel to a crowned cartoon rat.

She shut her eyes to the heat. *Cartoon rats. Rats in my dreams, rats in my bed. All hail King Rat. Long may he scurry through the gutters of the world. Immune to the very pestilence he spreads. Breeding death and discontent as he slithers past. King Rat, hateful of every victim he is denied. King Rat, gorging and still ravenous, scuttles ever closer, ever hungry. Now in the pipes and now in your bed. King Rat gnaws at your sleeping ear. So that you might not gauge the filth he gathers in the nights.*

Something touched her knee and she jolted awake.

Aurora, the day nurse said. Lunch time.

•

Will your daughter come today? Rora?

She licked her dry mouth and blinked. I don't know. I don't know. She, ah, said it was getting harder to move around. The Guardia Civil.

Of course. Like the old days.

71

Yes. *Those long years under the dictator's voice. The first rock albums on smuggled cassettes. Then the patrols gone and the tourists in their trooping mobs instead. The shoreline enshadowed by tower blocks, the mountains mutilated behind the concrete. Strange new food in the shops. Brightly boxed cereal. One bite sweet enough to loosen the teeth from your gum. Children crying foreign tears, red faces and strange tongues, their spilled ice cream tempting ants to the sunlight.*

Aurora?

Hmm?

I say like the old days. Checkpoints. A reason and a writ to go anyplace.

Yes, Aurora said. Yes. Perhaps it will be only for a little while. It's different this time of course.

The woman in the bed sniffed. A different face, giving the same orders.

Aurora patted her hand. Getting worked up does no good, eh?

Sirens on the highway. A useless wail in the forlorn streets of the world.

•

The man in the smock stepped into the staff room and sighed as he measured out coffee grounds and then shook them into the urn. The radio was on, and he listened to the host's unwavering voice. He heard a noise behind him and he turned to see Samper hunched over the back window, smoking.

You'll catch hell they hear'a you smoking in here.

Fuck it, Samper said. Makes no difference any more.

He took a step and turned down the radio. What?

I was listening to that, Samper said.

You wasn't serious about that shit? With the rest of them?

Samper shrugged.

It's lunacy.

We can't save them. They sure as shit won't be able to save themselves.

You don't need to though, not yet.

Samper lifted his chin toward the radio, exhaled smoke. Haven't you heard? It's closing in Alfi. They can't save anyone. All we can do is get out while roads are still open.

Christ above, Alfonse said. Just stop and think.

Samper wagged a finger at the silent radio. You hear the numbers today? Climbing. Fucking climbing. Best thing to do for them, triple their dosage, send 'em out numb. Before they have to live through s'more of, of this shit.

What are you going to do?

My family are in Teruel.

There's nobody left if you quit, Samp. Something happens to me, they could all die.

They're talking about a fucking lockdown. I heard Madrid has already sent for the army. My mother needs help. How'll she feed herself, I catch that shit? My family or my job? That what you're asking? Is it? Say it out loud so I can hear? Eh? You think, Jesus, you think I get paid anywhere near enough to even consider that shit?

Your job?

It's too much. It's too much.

These people are someone's mother, Samp, somebody's family.

And where are they huh? Where are the families?

The quarantines, how can they?

Always the right words, Alfi, eh? He turned and flicked the cigarette out of the window. It sailed down the building for an age until the wind flared and scattered sparks into the blue light of the evening. This thing is beyond fucking words.

We're gonna all be in the shit soon enough, all of us, and you're asking me to comfort these relics? Half of them don't even know what fucking year it is.

Please. It's a death sentence. Please.

Samper shook his head. No. Fuck you, my friend. That's not on me.

Samp.

Fuck you. Don't try and fucking guilt me, like you're some fucking priest. I'm going, before I can't.

Listen, Alfonse said, as his cellular phone began to ring, shrill and tinny. Wait. I think, you should——

What, I should what? Always with the fucking opinions, Samper said, and he waved a hand dismissively. Keep 'em to yourself. I don't need to hear all've your thoughts. Keep 'em to yourself. Eh? Maybe every one of your little fucking witterings don't need to be given oxygen. Eh? Maybe?

Samper.

Fuck off.

Alfonse shrank back as Samper flung open the door and went swearing down the corridor, the hydraulic door closing slow and softly behind him.

•

Aurora rubbed her back until she stopped.

Now come on, Suzi. Come on now. Didn't you want the truth? You always said you wanted the truth. Eh? Didn't you? Not to let a priest near you, even if you dived into the deep end? Hmm?

The other woman patted her eyes, nodded.

This is it, Suzi. They're gone now. I'm certain now. They aren't coming back.

They will. Why wouldn't they?

Aurora pressed her dentures with her tongue and put her open palm on the other's lap. Amor, she said. The tele and the radio. Beneath papery skin she felt the abraded bones of the woman's knee. *How like a sparrow she is.* We will get it with the rest of them. *My sparrow.*

Have you been down the hall?

No, Aurora said.

I thought I heard you. In the night.

No, Aurora said and *recalled the stench from the dayroom and the waste backed up in the toilet and nearly slipping on it and the nurses' station abandoned and the dispensary abandoned and the entire eastern corridor like the innards of a sewer pipe and the stairwell door that wouldn't budge even an inch and poor Tomas going up the hall mumbling and coughing, covered in shit to one elbow and blood to the other, a demented Christ emerged from the sewers.*

What will we do Rora?

Just try sleep some. I'll do the same. Take a drink. She patted the other woman's hand. There now. Aurora watched her drink, and then she lifted her own glass. Take some more, she said. Take some more, and I'll do the same.

In her dream the grass was wet and cool beneath her feet. The mansion loomed huge across the watered lawns and the ornate fountain. A champagne flute discarded at her feet as a powerful car roared down the gravel drive. She stood alone in the middle of a grand party. Her clothes were ragged and she was ashamed and she stood separate from the others in the middle of a vast and high-ceilinged room, unable to follow any of the conversations and filled by an immense ache of loneliness that set her sobbing. Someone pushed into her and as she was turned from the force her eyes caught the cold diamond light of the chandelier that seemed to lift and shimmer and to fade and to fade and to fade.

Stephen O'Donnell is a writer, living in Dublin, Ireland. His short stories have appeared most recently in *Underland Arcana*, *Strange Horizons*, and *Typehouse*.

Twitter: @stizzleodizzle

Website: http://bit.ly/stizzle0dizzle

A LETTER TO MY LEFT ARM

by Heidi Greco

D ear LA,

Please forgive the many disparaging things I have said about you over the years. I know, I've suggested you're kind of useless, that you're not as strong as my overly-used right arm, and that you don't even allow me to write legibly. I admit that I've sometimes labelled you as simply 'decorative' but oh, you are so much more than mere decoration.

You're my balance, my equalizer, and you're oh-so-very-brave.

Long ago, when the world was in another pandemic, you were the one who came to my defense. That time it wasn't a flu, but a horror called infantile paralysis—or, as it was more commonly known, polio.

I remember it as the summer when pretty much no one was allowed to swim at a public pool, as pools were where so many people caught the disease. It was an illness that killed people—one of the doctors in our town, a man who had a big family, unintentionally brought the disease back home and two of his six children died. I was horrified and frightened, and cried myself to sleep for nights.

Many of those who survived the disease were left paralyzed, some needing to live out their lives in a metal device called an iron lung, a machine that allowed them to breathe. The more fortunate survivors went on to lead normal lives, though they often required at least leg braces and crutches. One of the jobs I had while I was at university was in the office of a woman who used a wheelchair; her life had changed when as a teenager (and cheerleader) she'd contracted polio. She considered herself one of the lucky ones, as she'd married, had a loving husband and two wonderful kids, and beyond all that, had a very good job.

But back to the summer of that long-ago semi-lockdown. When Dr. Jonas Salk announced that he'd successfully developed a vaccine, everyone was eager to line up their kids for it. You and I, dear Left Arm, even managed to get our photo on the news, standing in line at the local public school, waiting for the nurse to give us our injection. It's only now, years later, I've learned that Dr. Salk refused to take a patent on the serum, deciding instead to not make any profit from it—all so it would be more widely available to people around the world. And now, while it's wonderful that scientists have managed to create more than one vaccine for COVID-19, it's hard to imagine that the corporations producing these drugs might practise such selflessness as Salk's. After all, too often we hear that a single dose of a pill to treat some rare disease can cost over a million dollars.

I'm glad, dear Left Arm, that you were so strong and brave when you took that free needle to protect me from polio. Just as now I can only thank you again—this time for your willingness to take the first jab of the new vaccine. I saw the way you lolled afterwards, growing pink and hot, and I did my best to soothe you with a cooling ice pack. So I'm hoping you'll still trust me when it's our turn for the second one (and oh, I can only hope you'll still be willing when the time comes for us to get follow-up injections). Likewise, I am crossing my fingers (on both hands) that costs for such shots won't be prohibitive—for anyone on the planet.

I'm sure there will be other diseases that will require inoculations for the safety of me and those I come in contact with. For whenever that might be, I'm counting on you to be there, for me and for them. So again, dear LA, I extend my apologies—not only from me, but also from my selfishly superior-acting right arm. From now on, I promise, we're going to appreciate you.

With love (and happy to be able to type with both hands!),
Heidi

Heidi Greco has lived on Canada's west coast since 1970. With writing in many genres, her books span poetry, fiction, and, most recently, non-fiction, with a book that takes a non-academic look at one of her favourite films, *Harold and Maude*. There's more at her website, heidigreco.ca.

LETHE'S SHARE

by Carsten Schmitt

had never been to a better place to perform *our* last rites. The hospice lobby smelled of the dried rose petals that filled tastefully arranged heavy glass bowls. The exposed oak beams and pinewood wall panels were reminiscent of a Bavarian inn. It was nothing like the other places, the state-run, merit-point-based clinics that were all beige walls and auto-nurses, the sour smell of decay covered barely by the odor of bleach and disinfectants.

The soft carpet silenced my steps as I crossed the lobby to approach the front desk. The receptionist looked up and smiled reflexively.

"Can I help you?" she asked.

"My name's Daniel Richter. I called earlier."

Her eyes unfocused as she called up the information on her smartlenses.

"Welcome, Herr Richter. I see *you* are on the sun terrace at the moment. Shall I call someone to take you there?"

I nodded, and she started talking to the air, her eyes unfocused again, "Hey, can you come and take Herr Richter to the sun terrace? Thanks."

Two minutes later, we were joined by a tall man, whose hair was done in tiny braids that bounced jauntily with every step. He, too, smiled at me, but his sentiment was warm and sincere. "Herr Richter? Please come with me. I'll take you to *you*."

We walked through corridors designed to maintain the facade of a gasthaus, right down to the fake deer antlers on the wall and oil paintings showing mountain scenery and pastoral motifs of centuries past.

"How am *I* feeling?" I asked the nurse, whose name I hadn't quite caught.

"Not great, but today isn't so bad. *You're* having a hard time keeping solid food down, so we supplement with IVs. But *you're* out in the fresh air as often as *you* feel up to it."

The corridor had three doors on either side. The middle one on the right opened when we passed it. A woman who looked like she was in her late twenties stepped out of the room. Her eyes were red-rimmed, and she stifled a sob when she hurried past us, barely acknowledging our existence.

"Some take it harder than others," my guide said. I nodded and braced myself for what was to come. It had become easier over time to see *me* die, but I still dreaded the sight.

•

I emerged from the semi-darkness of the hospice corridor into the amber light of a September afternoon that smelled of pinesap and hay drying on the meadows.

I pulled up a chair and sat down next to *my* sun bed. Despite the warm day, someone had covered *my* body with a white blanket. The wooden beam that propped up the roof of the sun terrace cast a shadow over my face that mercifully softened the deep lines that rapid decay had carved into *my* features. *I* almost looked like an elderly man having a nap.

The nurse gently touched *my* shoulder, and *I* awoke there on the sunbed, eyes blinking.

"Cannot see well," *I* said.

"Let's prop *us* up." I fumbled with the backrest, muttering a curse when it wouldn't budge.

"Allow me to help." The nurse pressed a small lever and adjusted the back.

"Thank you, Busa…" I began, trying to pronounce the syllables on his name tag.

"Boo-sahj-jah," he helped me.

"Busajja. I'm sorry."

"Never mind." He flashed a smile. "I'll leave you alone now. If you need me, just press the button on the armrest and I'll come."

"Thank you."

Busajja nodded and left us alone.

"*We* like him," *I* said.

"Yes, *we* do. Are they taking good care of *us*?"

I tried to answer, but only a racking cough came out of *my* mouth. "Water," *I* croaked.

A carafe stood on a small teak table next to the sun bed. The glass was misted with condensation and cool to the touch. Ice cubes clinked when I poured some water into a tumbler.

"Here," I said and leaned down to raise the glass to *my* lips. *I* drank with tiny sips, but still some liquid dribbled out of the corners of *my* mouth.

"Better now?"

I nodded weakly. "Won't get any better than this."

I didn't answer. What could I say? *I* was dying, and it showed. *My* forehead glistened with sweat, and *my* breath rattled in irregular bursts from hollow cheeks. How much time did *I* have left? Days at the most, maybe just hours. I had seen this before, and I was grateful for the idyllic surroundings. Good medical coverage and social status not only allowed *us* to live on indefinitely but also provided the means to ease any survivor's guilt.

"Listen," *I* said, and pointed shakily towards the vista below. Between the pine trees on either side, the view opened up to the village of Schliersee, its whitewashed houses and the bell tower of St. Sixtus silhouetted against the glitter of the lake and the Alps behind. "Can *we* hear it?"

I closed my eyes and listened. The warm Foehn wind carried tatters of tinny music and laughter—the unmistakable melody of a funfair.

"It must be a kirmess," I said, and with that realization came childhood memories of carousels and carnival games, the smell of candied almonds, and the cold sting on my incisors when I bit off the ice cream against my parents' sensible yet unheeded advice. When I got older, a teenager, the adrenaline-fueled thrill of the more exciting rides pushed away the simple joy of carousels, the taste of sticky sweets replaced by the pleasant buzz of my first sneaky drink of beer. It felt like forever since I had last been to a fair like that. That must have been just after my 18th birthday, when... I opened my eyes and chuckled.

"*Our* last kirmess. That was when *we* kissed..."

"Irene Adelberg," *we* both said at the same time.

"Well, it turned into a little more than a kiss, didn't it?"

"God, *we* haven't thought about her in a long time." It was good to see *me* laugh, to see a little color returning to *my* face.

"Yeah. Damn, she was pretty, and the only girl in school who loved grunge the way *we* did. She was cool."

"And so out of *our* league."

"Good thing she didn't care about that, eh?"

When I shut my eyes, I could see her, her face so close to mine I could feel her breath on my cheeks and savor the smell of the sun in her dirty-blonde hair. There was her mocking smile again when she said, "You gonna kiss me now, or what?" The mischievous glint in her eyes that turned my knees into rubber.

"What color were her eyes?" I asked.

"Her eyes?"

"Yes, do *we* remember?"

"*We*—" *My* answer drowned in a coughing fit that shook *my* body in spasmodic convulsions that wouldn't stop. Red-tinted saliva sprayed from *my* mouth and sprinkled specks of crimson onto the blanket.

I couldn't do much more than hold a tissue to *my* mouth and press the alarm. "There, there," I murmured. "Busajja will be here any moment."

The nurse came and pressed a med-jet injector to *my* neck. The hacking subsided, but the attack had left *me* exhausted.

"It is better you go now, Herr Richter," said Bussajja. "*You* need some rest."

"I have a room down in the village. Will you call me when I can come see *me* again?" He nodded, and I left *myself* in Busajja's care and returned to the car.

On the drive back to the inn, all I could think of was Irene's face, but no matter how hard I tried I couldn't recall the color of her eyes.

•

The thing I remember best, after I had decided to live forever, wasn't dying for the first time. It was in the spring of 2056, and I don't recall the passing—I remember the waking-up. It was what being born must feel like, my senses attacked by glaring lights and unfamiliar sounds, my skin susceptible to every little draft in the air and sudden change of temperature. Voices boomed in my ears, and hands propped me up and turned my head so that the colorless goo I retched up wouldn't splatter all over me. It tasted like raw egg white.

When I came to again, I was lying in a bed. Professor Fuchs was there, with two of his junior assistant doctors. "How do you feel, Herr Richter?" he asked. He looked like a walrus, with his drooping eyelids and the bushy mustache that covered his upper lip.

"Well enough, I guess."

"Excellent. All the tests we have run so far show that the procedure went just swimmingly."

He extended his hand, and one of the assistant doctors, a young woman with a ponytail and black-rimmed smartglasses, handed him a tablet. He brought up an image and turned the screen so I could see it. It looked like a UV-lit bundle of art yarn, dyed in fluorescent blues, greens, purples, and pinks. The image was 3D and rotated slowly. Professor Fuchs tapped the screen and what was one bundle became two, spinning at the same speed.

"This is your connectome, the entirety of all the synaptic connections your brain has formed during its life. This is *you*."

"It looks beautiful."

"It does, does it not?" Professor Fuchs beamed with pride. "As you can see," he pointed to a bar chart on the display, "we have achieved a match of 99.9843 percent."

"So, there's a loss?"

"Lethe's Share," the assistant doctor murmured. Fuchs gave her an irritated look but continued as if he had heard nothing. "Technically, it's not one hundred percent complete but as good as. Nothing you will notice, anyway. Most of your memories are fabricated, did you know that? The brain fills in the bits it has forgotten, interpolates the gaps. But the important things—your personality—are all there. I can guarantee you that."

"Will this happen every time I move to a new body?"

"Unfortunately, yes. It's likely less than what would occur naturally during a lifetime, but there will inevitably be some loss. That's why keepsakes are so important. Photos or tangible mementos help to establish a strong sense of continuity. As does a healthy network of friends and family. Do you have family?"

"My wife died before all of this was available."

"I am sorry to hear that. Anybody else?"

"My daughter, Julia, her husband, and my grandchildren. We are pretty close."

"Very good. Have you left your daughter's contact details? We will let her know everything is fine."

That was when it hit me for the first time that the person who legally was my daughter, had been fathered by another man, a man who was waiting somewhere in this building, waiting for me to come and say good-bye.

•

When I met *myself* that first time, the "real" me—although the Transition Counselor never tired of telling me I shouldn't think that way—he, *I*, had already lost all legal claims to *our* life. For the span of a few days, before I was fully awake and certified good-to-go, *I* had been denied any contact with the outside world, *our* accounts frozen, everything suspended, waiting for me to pick it all up again.

We were two persons during that brief period of time for which our memories wouldn't match. I sometimes wonder if *I* had harbored doubts, whether *I* ever questioned the decision to create me. If so, *I* never told me. I think *we* were both still uncomfortable with the whole situation.

"Will you look after Julia?" *I* asked.

"Yes, I, *we*, will. She is *our* daughter, and *we* love her very much."

I closed my eyes and sighed, and then asked me to get it over with, because, yes, *I* was a little afraid. There was a white pillbox on the nightstand. I opened it, shook out the cornstarch wafer that was inside, reached down, and placed it on *my* tongue.

When it was over, I looked for a window, but the room didn't have one, only a screen showing a green meadow under an azure sky with algorithmically generated cloud patterns. I suppose that was good because if it had been real, I might have opened it. The Transition Counselor would not have approved.

In the parking lot, I called Julia.

"How are you feeling, Dad?"

"I don't know. Weird. Sad."

"That's normal. I remember my first time. It was pretty rough. I'm glad you did it, though."

"Me too, I guess."

•

Every time my ten-year rebirth plan came up for renewal, I underwent the same procedure. A fresh body had been grown from the DNA sample I had provided, accelerated gestation bought at the expense of reduced longevity, and every time, they made a new copy of my connectome. Every time, some doctor would run tests, ask me questions, and show me how well the transfer had worked. I never paid much attention to the accuracy of connectome matches. They consistently stayed within the 99 percent range, and I experienced no memory glitches. None that I noticed, anyway.

Now, lying on this twentieth-century monster of a bed in my room at the inn, staring at the wood-paneled ceiling, I wondered whether failing to remember Irene's eye color was normal. Had I forgotten it even before I had begun to live in ten-year intervals, like I had forgotten the names of the kids I used to play with in kindergarten? I hadn't thought about Irene in a long time and maybe it had been erased by the memories of other women.

I could hear the fair through the open window, and the sounds carried my mind back to that night so long ago. It nagged at me, made me wonder how many other details had sunk into the sediment of lost memories, forgotten not through the natural erosion of time, but by trying to hold on to them.

"Cloud! Find Irene Adelberg, from Munich, Bavaria, born 1979. Images only."

The ubiquitous Cloud picked up my command and projected a raster of images onto my lenses. I flipped through row after row of photos but found none that resembled her. Would I even recognize her? Had she gone dark, shielded behind heavy privacy settings? Or maybe she had passed away, her family refusing to maintain a public memento? These days everybody felt a little awkward admitting the possibility of death.

This wasn't getting me anywhere, so I decided to do the one thing the Counselors had repeatedly warned me not to do. I had to ask *myself* as long as I still had the chance.

•

Busajja had taken me back to my room, the last I would ever call home. Before I went to Schliersee, the Transition Counselor had recommended bringing a few personal items to soften the foreignness of my new surroundings. She had meant well, but the picture of Kathrin in the silver frame felt oddly misplaced on the nightstand next to the fragrant flower bouquet that was replaced every couple of days. My wife had never liked cut flowers. She had hated how they had been killed merely to embellish someone's living room.

I didn't bring much more than that, save my favorite wool blanket that Busajja had now drawn up to my shoulders and a yellowed drawing in crude green, blue, and yellow wax crayon that Julia had made one rainy afternoon on vacation in Brittany. She used to draw pictures with such joy we joked she'd become an artist someday. Ultimately, she became a lawyer, but I had kept her drawings.

My eyesight had deteriorated further. I blinked, yet I could barely make out the picture that the nurse had tacked to the wall. Above it, a framed print boasted an aphorism in squiggly writing.

"Busajja?"

"Yes, Herr Richter?"

"Please, call me Daniel."

I could hear the smile in his voice. "Okay, Daniel. What is it?"

"Will you sit with me for a while?"

He pulled a chair next to my bed. He sat down, close, but his body was just a blurry silhouette of shadows and bright lines painted by the sunlight falling through the venetian blinds. I could feel his hand warm and dry on mine.

"That writing on the wall. What does it say again?"

"*The life of the dead is placed in the memory of the living,*" he said.

"Who is that by?"

"Cicero, the Roman philosopher."

"Do you know Cicero?"

"I wrote an essay about him in college."

"You studied Classics?"

"Philosophy."

"How did you end up in this job then?"

"I got into it for the points, initially, but then I realized that working here is applied philosophy, so I stayed."

"I'm sorry, I didn't mean to..." I trailed off. What did I not mean to? Remind him I was living and being reborn on the privileged side of life? Busajja had been here for me, night and day since I got here... when? A week ago, maybe two? Yet I knew so little about him.

"What do you think? Was Cicero right?"

Busajja took his time to think before answering.

"I guess," he said. "It's our memories that make us who we are. When we pass them on, we live on."

"I wonder how Cicero could be so certain. They didn't have cloning and Connectome transfers back then."

"No, they didn't. But they had their heirs and loved ones to remember them. That's not so bad."

"And yet you are saving points for a plan."

"I am, but not for me. The points are for my sister. She's alone and not very close to anybody." There was regret in his voice.

"Why are you doing this for her?"

"She's not a bad person, just... very sad. Maybe one day she'll heal and find some happiness in this life."

"What about you?" I asked.

"I have two daughters. I hope they will remember me. The good bits at least." Busajja laughed his baritone laugh.

"I'm sure they will. As will I, if for a little while."

"But remember, only the good bits!" He chuckled.

"Only the good bits," I promised.

•

I didn't hear Busajja leave. He held my hand in his until I fell asleep, and when I woke up in my dream, it had become Irene's.

We had stayed the whole afternoon at the fair, going on the rides with the blasé attitude of teenagers who'd rather die than admit we enjoyed them like when we were kids. And we probably didn't, since we were too absorbed by each other's presence. Every turn of the carousel and every push and shove in the throng of people was an excuse to touch each other as if by accident.

When we had had enough, I bought two bottles of beer, and we walked through the quiet town, just us and the bats chasing the moths orbiting the yellow streetlights. We held hands, drank beer, and talked about what we would do after we'd graduate from high school next year.

"I'll walk you home," I said finally, relieved I got out the words with barely a tremor in my voice.

Her parents owned a fancy house, all straight angles of steel and concrete with windows that went from floor to ceiling. More importantly, they were away for the weekend.

By the time we arrived at her door, my last ounce of courage had seeped out of me, pumped through every pore of my body by my frantically beating heart. I stood and looked at her and didn't know what to say or do.

"You gonna kiss me now, or what?"

To this day, I don't know what I would have done, had she not asked. We kissed, clumsily at first, like someone walking on unknown ground but eager to explore. She fumbled for her keys, not separating her lips from mine.

The next thing I remember was lying beside her, looking into her eyes and feeling her breast cupped in my hand, gingerly caressing it through the soft fabric of her t-shirt.

"Do you want me to take that off?" she asked, tugging at her t-shirt.

I nodded.

"Give me a hand, will you?"

I did, and then I took off my shirt, too. She pulled me to her, and I could feel her cool skin on mine. We kissed, blindly unfastening belts and zippers, wriggling out of suddenly too-tight jeans, trying to reconcile all the theoretical knowledge from SexEd and school yard talk with the reality of the moment.

We managed pretty well.

•

When I opened my eyes, I studied Irene's sleeping face in front of me on the pillow we shared. Her hair was tousled, and her mouth was open just a bit so I could not resist kissing her, biting her lower lip teasingly.

She woke up, yawned, and stretched like a cat.

"Good morning," I said. "Sleep well?"

She nodded, not yet willing to open her eyes to the dawn light. We hadn't closed the blinds the night before—there hadn't been time for that.

"Breakfast's your job," she mumbled, and then, when I wouldn't get up, "What's the matter?"

"Nothing. Just looking at you."

She rolled onto her back and stretched again, fully aware that I was watching her.

"Well, you better get me a jam toast real quick, or you'll never see any more of this, my friend."

I kept looking at her, willing to defy her for just one more minute, when the taste of iron filled my mouth. A spasm clenched my chest, and I coughed until I could feel blood running down my chin and spat out lumps of lung tissue. Gray nothingness replaced Irene's face, and I couldn't hear anything but white noise buzzing in my ears.

I reached for the emergency wristband and squeezed it with what strength I had left.

Busajja came a moment later. He propped me up in bed so I wouldn't choke on my own blood and wiped my chin with a damp cloth. His voice tunneled through the noise in my ears: "It's all right, Daniel. I'm here, I'm here."

"I think it's time," I croaked.

"Yes, Daniel. I'll call *you*. *You* will be here in no time, and then you can go. Everything will be alright."

I heard him pick up the med-jet on the nightstand.

"Don't." I shook my head. "I want to be awake."

Busajja was talking to someone. My mind drifted again, and there was Irene's face. She opened her eyes, and I could see their green irises. I hadn't forgotten. Was I to be the last in an endless succession of Daniel Richter copies to know about Irene Adelberg's pale green eyes? Was their memory the only thing that made me *me*? And if I told the other Daniel, would he *remember*?

•

I wished the BMW could ignore the speed limit. The car, however, didn't and stuck to a maddeningly law-abiding 30 kph on the way to the hospice. Busajja had phoned early in the morning. The nurse's voice had been calm, yet I could sense the urgency.

"You should come. It's time."

I disconnected the call, got dressed, and was on my way in less than five minutes.

Busajja met me at the entrance and led me to *my* room. I knew what awaited me inside, but even the routine couldn't quite dampen the shock. *I* looked worse than yesterday, sweat covering *my* face and neck, *my* eyes wide open, unblinking.

"*You* cannot see, but *you* can hear, Daniel."

I barely registered his use of my first name and crossed the room to *my* bed.

"You've come," *I* said.

"Sure… *we've* never let any of *us* go alone, have *we*?"

"No, *we* haven't."

My breathing was shallow and labored, and I looked for Buasajja, waiting by the door. He nodded and handed me a plastic pillbox. Inside, I would find a corn starch wafer drenched with painless death.

"Do you want me to stay?" he asked.

Feeling I would choke up, I merely shook my head.

"I'll leave you alone then. Call me when… just call me."

He left, and *we* were alone. "Remember what *we* were talking about yesterday? The kirmess? Irene, and *our* first kiss?"

I nodded almost imperceptibly.

"*We've* been thinking. *We* don't have any photos of her, and it's been driving *us* crazy. *We* tried to remember her eyes, and the memory is there, almost in *our* reach if *we* try just hard enough, but *we* can't grasp it. I mean, how could *we* forget such a thing?"

I blinked, as if to tell me *I* understood.

"*We* wondered if…" I hesitated. "*I* wondered if *you* remembered."

His lips moved, but I couldn't hear what he said, so I leaned closer. "Blue. Her eyes were blue." And just like that the memories returned. Of course, she'd had those sky-blue eyes I had not permitted myself to like at first because, c'mon—blonde and blue-eyed?—that would have been too cliché to be cool. It had all come back now.

"Thank you. It means a lot to me."

"You're welcome." He smiled softly, voice barely audible. "Will you do me the honors?"

I opened the container, took out the wafer with my thumb and index finger, and carefully placed it on his tongue. "Rest now."

I stayed and held his hand until the end. When he had stopped breathing, I got up and opened the window for him.

•

The BMW announced an incoming call. "Answer," I said, and an image of Julia formed on the dashboard screen.

"Hi, Dad!"

"Hello, Love."

"How are you?"

She had offered to come with me, just to stay at the inn so I wouldn't be alone when it was all over. I had explained to her that I'd rather be on my own, and she had understood. She never wanted anyone to accompany her on one of these trips.

"I'm okay, I guess. *We*... he and I, could talk before the end, and it was peaceful."

"That's good. I just wanted to be sure you're all right."

"I am."

She smiled. "I love you. See you later."

"I love you, too. Oh... Julia?"

"Yes, Dad?"

"Your mother's eyes," I began.

"What about them?"

"Do you remember what color they were?"

Carsten Schmitt was born on a decidedly un-stormy April afternoon in 1977. He spent his childhood exploring the forests, derelict coal mines, and bunkers around his home town. When those exploits became too boring, he extended his exploring to faraway planets and fantastic worlds in his imagination. He never lost his love for speculative literature and took up writing his own stories as a teenager. After a long hiatus, he returned to writing in 2016 and has since published stories in anthologies such as *Der Unmögliche Mord* and *Wie Künstlich ist Intelligenz?*

Carsten was awarded the Deutscher Science Fiction Preis (German Science Fiction Award) for Best Short Story of 2020 and was a finalist for George R. R. Martin's Terran Award. He is an alumnus of the 2018 Taos Toolbox writing workshop, run by Walter Jon Williams and Nancy Kress in New Mexico.

Carsten lives with his partner and three fluffy cats in Saarbrücken, in the Saarland region of Germany. You can find him online at www.carstenschmitt.com or @CarsTheElectric on Twitter.

ALCHEMY

by Helen Bowie

After the battles of our youth, there are no reliable narrators left among us. To crystallise each memory as truth would hurt too much. We can never be miners searching for the diamonds that lie beneath—deep down we fear the excavation will bring us nothing more than poisoned lead. So we become alchemists. We take what we find, and put it through the process of reminiscence, until we are left with pure gold, reflecting light back into our eyes so strongly that it blinds us.

As we emerge from our depths and share stories, of the men who followed us home, buzzed every flat on the street, preyed on our vulnerability through unsolicited patisserie and a listening ear at 4am, to the demons within, those tricyclics and dark forms cast away or kept at bay but never truly bested, we reform the poison until it sparkles.

Through the sorcery of lives well lived, our coven transmutes these matters, our greatest power, the one they could not take from us, the one we take from them, and through our commune, our laughter, these base metals—the foundations of the women we have become—take on new life, no longer trauma bonds, but a universal elixir, to heal the eternal youth we find in our reminiscences, to take the pain away.

Blast the heavy metals of your traumas into glorious glitter. Apply your glitter as warpaint. Take on the world once more.

Helen Bowie (they/them) is a writer, performer, and charity worker based in London, England. Their writing is inspired by bad politics, good make-up, and average life experiences. Their debut collection of interactive and experimental writing, *WORD/PLAY*, is available now from Beir Bua Press. Helen is extremely online on twitter @helensulis.

THE PRETERITIONS

by Benjamin Gardner

The war was old and both sides were tired of fighting. I had been traveling over the border in a bohemian town. I thought I would be safe, but I was apprehended as a spy and was imprisoned soon after. The guards at the prison didn't even care about the war, and they mostly let me do what I wished. They often talked to me because they were bored, and it helped pass the time. The prison was isolated; I tried to escape once, but the guards found me wandering in the moors. I'd lost my sense of direction and had no idea where to go.

I found out about *The Preteritions* from one of the guards. We talked about books in the long days of summer. He was a collector, and his friend had given him a copy of *The Preteritions,* neatly bound in leather with a strap to tie it shut.

I was one of three prisoners at the prison. Deccan and Aisha were both pilots, and I was, more or less, a civilian who happened to be from the same country as the two pilots. We all tried to get along with one another, and, for the most part, we succeeded.

The guards treated us fairly. There were four of them most of the time. We ate the same things they ate even though the food was too bland for my taste. Deccan raved about the food, but Aisha agreed that it could use more spice and heat. We played football and backgammon with the guards too. Aisha and I would take walks around the premises inside the high brick walls that separated us from the moorland. If a supervisor was visiting, we'd stay in our cells, but otherwise we walked freely on the grounds.

I read *The Preteritions* from cover to end in a single day. The guard brought it to me in the fall. I know because I remember that it had started getting cold in the evenings. His friend Edwin (though I don't remember the guard's name) collected artifacts from Siberia and Lapland. Edwin bought sacred objects from a former shaman from Siberia, and she had sold him the book, saying that it was a book of a religion that was not hers. Edwin had given it to the guard as a gift because he collected old books. Another of the guards said he had heard of the text before. He said that it was a quack book that his grandparents talked about when he was young, but his dad had always told him it was meaningless.

The guard knew I was an avid reader and enjoyed many types of books, so he brought *The Preteritions* to show me one day. It really was quite an extraordinary book. I recognized the language almost immediately, and the guard also claimed to know some of the passages (despite not being able to read it outright) and had gotten far enough to know that it was of some religious import. It was interesting to read a text that hovered on the edge of memory for so many people. Even if they were unable to read the language, we all recognized passages as they had been told to us by our grandparents.

Deccan and Aisha were also curious about the book. Deccan could not read the text, but Aisha was able to translate some words individually. A few days after the guard brought the book, I proposed that we work together to translate it, and, to my surprise, everyone agreed.

I am not a translator but have great interest in Peter Ladefoged's work documenting phonetic sounds of endangered languages. I have always had a fondness for language as a representation of cultures different from my own and learned as many as I could, through travel and books. I needed a project to focus on in prison and was glad that Aisha and Deccan were also interested.

The language is probably not one that you are familiar with, so I should tell you what I know about it and the people who used it. It is probably not spoken very often these days, but suffice it to say that I believe it to be a sort of Finno-Ugric language, likely closest to Saamic, which made sense if the guard's friend collected art objects from Laplanders (which, to my understanding, is an offensive term to the Sámi). I had read Johan Turi's book *Muitalus samiid birra* after finishing college as a means to learn the language. It had been awhile since I had looked at it, but I found myself relearning the poetry of the language quickly as I read the guard's book to Deccan and Aisha.

Here's the thing, though: I did not believe the book was written by a Sámi. Before translating it, I suspected it was written by someone involved with some proto-Gnostic religion. After finishing the project, I was even more confused about who wrote the text and why it was presented in Sámi. Aisha suggested it was distributed as a religious pamphlet, and I agreed with her assertion because nothing else really made sense.

It took Aisha and I approximately three years to translate. Deccan picked up the language fairly well too, saving us a number of months. Translated to English (the language the three of us could agree on, though we weren't happy about the choice) it was around two hundred and fifty pages. Though we certainly argued about certain passages, the project brought the three of us closer, and we took great pride in our work. It was the first language other than his born tongue that Deccan had learned, and his sense of achievement was visible. It was beautiful to see someone accomplish something that they did not think was possible. We kept the translated pages of *The Preteritions* in an old cardboard box in the corner of my cell.

We were released during the hot days of summer, about five years after we'd first been imprisoned. The prison was closing, and the guards expected to be transferred in a matter of days. Our government had negotiated our release, and we were driven to the border. I was forced to leave the translation with the guard when we left.

His promise to bring me the translation as soon as the war ended was not fulfilled because war still haunted our two countries, and I had heard of great atrocities carried out by both militaries. I had no idea what I would do with the translation, but I was saddened by the possibility that I may never see it again.

In the winter though, I started seeing flashes of text that I believed to be from the book. The mental images of the text came in violent dreams, preventing peaceful sleep and leaving me exhausted during the days. I had a hard time focusing on work. Most people were tired of life being a constant struggle, and I blended in well because my nightmares took any joy from everyday living.

There you are, waiting. We will just walk by.

Aisha and I had worked together since our release, collecting and distributing rations to help the war effort. We distributed food in three towns south of the border and collected metal and glass from the communities that could spare the materials.

Aisha, who was a ray of sunlight during our time in prison, seemed as ragged as me most days. I asked her if everything was okay.

"I'm not sleeping well," she said as we drove to Pellam, the town in the center of our daily route.

"Is something the matter?"

"I think it is just the war."

We didn't talk about it again, but some weeks later she came to work with a black eye. I asked her again if she was okay.

"I'm still not sleeping well."

"Did someone hit you?"

She turned up the volume on the short-wave radio, filling the vehicle with static, avoiding the question.

Passages from the book started coming to me in the middle of the day. If I found myself staring out the window of the car as we drove, words from the book would sit in the front of my mind, the empty landscape and bombed out buildings not much more than background to the original text and our translation.

With hope you look to the sky or down below, but we are right behind you.

War had made me agnostic, I believe, but *The Preteritions* spoke not of gods. It spoke of reality, I think. Not a religious reality, but rather an insight to something that we, as humans, were too close to see.

The next day, someone new picked me up to distribute food.

"Where is Aisha?"

"I don't know, my supervisor just told me to switch to this route today."

I was worried about Aisha. I didn't really take much time to get to know the new person. Their name was Tonyon. Driving between the border villages made me think about the text more. I would stare out the window while Tonyon drove between towns and fragments of the text would float on the landscape like soldiers.

There is no mystery to us. To you, all is cloaked in sadness and you chose to pretend it is a mystery. Our time is short, we will live beyond this world long after you have gone.

"What are you thinking about?" Tonyon asked between the villages one day.

I didn't answer. My mind was unraveling and connecting words as if they emerged from the blank landscape. Abandoned buildings and scrub grass bore *The Preteritions.* I did my best to recite the text that I remembered under my breath because I thought it might be the only way the book would exist.

At night, I would write the words I remembered on paper. I found an old, used folder at our headquarters and brought it home. I collected the papers that I penned every night. As the war seemed endless, I believed this would be another good project, something else to focus my energy on. It was most difficult to remember the order of the words, but the more I wrote, the easier it was to put everything in sequence.

The nightmares still came but less frequently. Mostly, I would dream of being stuck in the prison without guards, and I would smell smoke. I was the only one in the jail cell, and the loneliness hung over me like static from a television.

At the end of summer, more than a year after I'd been freed from prison, Tonyon asked if I attended church.

"No," I told them. "I don't see the point."

"Do you have a group which you belong to?"

"No."

"Why don't you come meet some friends of mine," they said.

I didn't answer. I figured not committing was the best approach.

Those who seek us will be ignored. Those we seek will not live.

I came home that night to find that my room had been broken into. My rations and clothing were taken. The folder was still underneath my bed, the place where I hid it every night, but it was empty except for a brief note.

> *Dear Landon,*
>
> *I dreamed that you had completed The Preteritions again. You are not meant to have this; it is not meant for us.*
>
> *XO,*
>
> *Aisha*

I felt nothing reading the note. I tried to sleep, but I had the most horrible dreams. Not of the jail, but of the roads and towns I visited every day with Tonyon. They were filled with monsters, humanoid creatures that looked like jumbles of body parts and animal appendages. I could feel the beasts tearing at my skin in my dreams and devouring my flesh as Tonyon watched. Before I awoke, I recognized the face of one of the beasts. A face I knew very well, except that it now had the mandibles of an insect and the horns of an elk protruding from his skull. Despite the mutations, it was the face of Deccan.

During our drive the next morning, Tonyon was in a particularly chatty mood. Having not slept much, I used my jacket as a pillow and tried to sleep while Tonyon droned on about something that did not interest me. Their words and tone were an incantation, soothing me to sleep as the vehicle rattled down the dusty road.

I dreamt, yet again, but this time the dream was sweet. Perhaps my soul had taken too much negative energy and this kind dream was all that remained, or perhaps Tonyon's chanting was in my favor. I was taking tea with Aisha and Deccan in the courtyard of the prison where we were discussing a book with the guards. We weren't discussing it, I guess, but rather reciting it, the whole thing, from start to finish. I knew that I would not be able to remember it, but I had so much joy in the dream. It was a perfect day as a memory, even if it hadn't ever been real.

I woke to the sound of an old wooden door's latch fastening. Burnt sage filled my nostrils, and my tongue felt raw as if I'd burnt it on something. It was dark, but I could see the calves of people standing around the room, illuminated by candles on the ground.

"Welcome, Landon."

"Tonyon?"

"I'm here too, Landon."

"We invited you here to recite the book to us. We will end the war with the book."

The voice was Deccan's. I could hear him reciting passages in the courtyard over tea.

We care nothing of your petty disagreements. We will destroy your world and pass you by.

"Tell us what you remember, Landon." Aisha said. "We will listen, and they will come."

A sudden pain in my shoulder made me attempt to stretch and realize I was tied to a plank of wood. I could faintly see windows in the room, illuminated by the light of the stars.

I started reciting what I remembered of the book, from the moment of our creation to the disregard that those that knew of our creation held for us. I recited the ways that the authors of the book tinkered with our dreams and that some of them found joy in causing us pain. I enumerated the foundations of reality laid out in the book. And, finally, I spoke the final chapters of reckoning.

With each phrase I remembered in the final chapters, the others in the darkened room intonated deep throaty sounds. The noises filled up my chest, and I felt the ground tremble beneath my feet. I could feel the world falling away as

I realized *The Preteritions* was never a book but rather an instruction manual. Deccan, Aisha, Tonyon, and the others invoked the omission of the world as I spoke the words I remembered. A great, green light filled the windows outside of the room, but I could not stop conveying the book as their chanting continued.

I spoke the last word I remembered from the book that had given my life so much meaning—not in its content, but because it gave me purpose—and I realized that I was alone in the room. The candles had burned down to the wick, and my arms were not bound to anything. I could see a faint, morning light coming through the windows which had seemed to have been an unearthly green only a moment before. The space became familiar as more and more light entered from the rising sun.

I opened the door and stepped out into the brisk, morning air. The prison stood alone in the middle of the moor. The outer brick wall had been destroyed, so I could see straight into the barren land. I was starving, and as I ate from the rations, I realized that I was surrounded by a great silence. I wondered if the war had finally stopped.

Benjamin Gardner is a writer and a multimedia artist living in the Midwestern United States. He is a founder and co-editor of Theurgical Studies Press which publishes limited edition risograph art zines. Gardner's artwork has been exhibited across the United States and he makes music as Asurta and Lost Music Library. His short fiction has been included in the *Mysterium Tremendum* zine and *Night Terrors Volume 4*. Gardner is also a Professor of Art and Design at Drake University, teaching classes on visual art and visual culture. More information is available at www.benjaminagardner.com.

THE ELDER TREE

by Shanon Sinn

He had stood for over 2000 years while all of those around him had fallen. He could still feel many of them splayed across the crowns of his bulging roots. Others remained as stumps throughout the fog-breathing forest, parents of thin saplings too young for him to yet acknowledge.

There were also the other trees—some several hundred years old now. None of them had his memories. They did not know the things he knew. Only the mycelium he shared the earth with could fathom all that he had seen and done.

The tree had been an antlered stag in rut, a hooting owl in the darkness, and a snake writhing beneath autumn leaves as it feasted upon mouthfuls of mammalian prey. He had been a songbird one hundred, hundred thousand times, a wolf cub curled up in the shadows, a crow in flight, and a hidden ancient thing too forbidden to name. He had been a lightning strike, a wailing storm, a drop of rain, and a single ray of sunlight in numbers infinite enough to be incomprehensible, even to him.

He had once been a man sleeping beneath a twisted blanket, dreaming of a woman who would one day give him sons. The tree's discarded branches had become fuel for the man's campfire, a poking stick for his coals, and thick smoke that chased away hordes of disease-ridden mosquitos with ill intent. His trunk kept the wind off of the man, along with the bitter harshness of late October dew. The eyes of the hunting cats too.

Ten million million ants had known the tree by his sentient name. A billion wasps. A trillion beetles. He had become one with all of them, and they had become one with him. Through them he had won dominion over the forest, claiming great stretches of territory as armies marched to war along pathways claimed by his carefully placed micro roots.

The tree king was god to forty-three different plant species, hundreds who lived in relationship with him even now, and tens of thousands who had already gone back into the earth. He had been all of them as well.

The Tree had been counsel to the stones that rested between the dominions of the Earth. Their messengers, the worms, had rubbed their sides along his buried roots, and the spores who built cities for the hidden ones upon his lichen-crusted chest had witnessed it all.

The Tree of all Trees had laughed, made love, and fought bitterly with too many winds to name—though every last one of them he remembered in minute detail. It had taken over a thousand years for Him to make contact with the far-off stars, each of them an auntie or uncle, proud Elders teaching him the secrets of distant galaxies.

The fungi had emptied out the dead parts that had grown inside of him, keeping him propped up for another two hundred and thirty-three years. Their orders had been sent out to the shrubs and the flowers and the berries and the grasses to dig deep into the crevasses of the other lords and ladies, to grasp and cling to one another, and to hold taut the trembling monsters of the Tree God's legs beneath them, now ancient and weary.

He slipped from the sky and fell into the moss-rich earth, leaving an echo that spread into the valleys and over the distant mountaintops. For all eternity.

Shanon Sinn is the author of *The Haunting of Vancouver Island*. His writing can also be found in Nelson's *Canadian Corrections* textbook, *The Times Colonist*, and in several other publications online and in print.

Shanon earned his Creative Writing degree at Vancouver Island University. There he received the Barry Broadfoot Award for Journalism and the Gisele Merlet Creative Writing Award. His focus at VIU was on First Nations topics. These included Elder teachings, field school at the University of Fairbanks in Alaska (learning oral history recording guidelines), and being an intern for Snuneymuxw Elder in Residence Geraldine Manson. He is interested in the Indigenous ghost stories of British Columbia, both authentic and colonial burial ground urban legends.

ILL SPIRITS

by Bryn Hammond

They hadn't called in a shaman to heal their sick man. A visitor came: Agyr-Anja, who had lost his wife to what presented as the same condition, with a leg rash and a fear of water. He advised them: "Don't dismiss it as an aggravated winter illness. The shamans up north had no doubt my wife was attacked by a spirit. They couldn't help. They said we had brought the ill spirit with us, it was a stranger to them and belonged to Merqot." He had been too far away to haul her home to a Merqot shaman, alive.

Even with his evidence, the winter-quarters community at Utaly Waters, fifteen men and women with eight children, spat out bones. Shamans were an unpredictable expense, and the sick man, their big hunter, had been out of action for three weeks. It was the tail-end of winter, stocks low. He'd rally in the spring, they said.

Agyr-Anja told them, "My wife was our backbone, and never lay sick in her life. She was the Old Doe of the herd, if I ever knew the equivalent in humans, and yet not old in years, either."

Still they talked of how strong their hunter was, how vigorous. Seeing they were reluctant to be taught by him, by the precedent of his dead wife that he had put before them, Agyr-Anja left.

The Utaly Waters community had been ashamed to admit to him why they hadn't consulted the shaman who spent the winter nearest, at Short Moss. One of them owed the Black Cloud Spirit from three years ago, after alleviation of his daughter's despair. Taigho Shaman would roast their toes about it. She wouldn't refuse service, but might insist on both payments.

By convention, a journey-shaman, who moved from place to place and took on clients at opportunity, did not demand as much in fees as a specific practitioner you called yourself. Journey-shamans—not those who lived in families or otherwise remained with a community—employed a gossip-bird to scour the area for news. These spies, in the shape of the commonest of common brown finches, flitted into a camp and overheard such circumstances of a case that let their shaman impress prospective clients with pre-knowledge. That happened here.

Qamty used masculine speech tags for himself and kept a curl of bristle on his chin, and he wore what was a woman's hat in Merqot, white stoat, with pearls and silver strung into his hair. His deer, the one he rode and the others under bags, six of them, were soft stags that had a doe's proportions. These were sacred creatures, but uneasy in a camp. The gossip-bird sat on his shoulder, and had chattered into his ear an inexplicable acquaintance with them, names and dates and need.

"Or else he met Agyr-Anja," went the mutter. But they congratulated themselves on a cheaper treatment, and they hired him.

A shaman can't communicate with spirits underground, in earthed-over winter quarters. Ahead of the night's performance, they set up a warm-weather tent, made of living things, with the cosmic symbols seared into the skins.

Meanwhile he ate. How much he foraged for himself at winter's end they didn't know—shamans don't kill animals, and depend on those who do—but he ate almost with a monstrous appetite, as if his stomach went down and down like a pit for frozen meat.

There did exist bad shamans, monsters in the guise of shamans who fed upon the souls they ought to save. A few of the community thought this as they watched him gorge.

His strange deer set a problem: their home herd already prowled around them with a hostile curiosity, and both had to roam overnight to feed. They agreed the children would go out with the strangers and lead them to moss at a distance from where their home deer browsed. As an advantage, this task took the children out of range of the shaman's activity.

Before he entrusted his animals to them, Qamty spoke to the children. "These are my kin, precious to me," he told them, and they nodded at least as seriously as he.

"We'll have sticks," said a young one, "and we'll take their side in trouble. Ours won't dare."

Pyrgy, the eldest girl, asked him what the adults wondered. They had seen him unload the wicker hutch he slept in, that sprang up like a trap, cased in skins. "Do you always travel on your own? Don't you have people? Aren't you lonely?"

"No. I have a husband. He's a spirit, and lives on—" he pointed a finger into the west quarter of the afternoon sky "—lives on the third star of the track in the Speedy Sled constellation. Besides, in a camp with other people I couldn't easily keep my soft stags. Have you noticed how in the wild they make a society themselves, the soft stags? Not necessarily the hard does."

"I have not seen a number of them together."

"We like each other's company." He included himself with the deer, being a 'soft man,' so-named for them. "And people give them to me, or such a one as me, when a sacred deer is cast in a home herd. Never a worse fate, I hope."

"Can we touch them?"

"If they offer. I have promised them they needn't be afraid of you, but several of them have a past of violence. Don't try to stroke their antlers. A soft stag keeps the mossy, ultra-sensitive skin an antler grows in, that a stag thinks himself well rid of. A hard doe's antlers do shed the soft, and branch into unfeeling weapons like a stag's."

"Do the other deer not know them sacred?"

"Rarely. Most deer find difference an affront—as stupid, exposed to a miracle, as most humans."

"They look too dainty to be riding-stags."

"Oh, I am the weight of a bird," answered the shaman.

They sent away the children—night advanced. Like deer, spirits slept by day and fed at night. Beginning to sing, the shaman fetched in his helper spirits. People finished their chores in unease. Two of the tunes they knew too well, and the spirits who answered to them—people muttered casual, derogatory names to disguise their dread: Crazy Pox, Aunty Blast. Once these spirits had been malignant, like the unknown that attacked them in the body of their hunter. They had body counts, these spirits; they had inflicted sickness on humans and on herds; they had bloody pasts. Now the shamans had tamed them and converted them to service—as if you harnessed a bear to pull your sled, when most people were content with dogs. That's a shaman for you.

Only Lashqat, a young singer, did not avoid the shaman as he sang the songs that were mostly nonsense to a human ear. Lashqat sat near and listened. He saw the shaman's manner, his expressions, heard his low endearments as his helpers came to him and frisked around him, invisible to human eyes. Lashqat hoped to court a young woman he had met in the tents on Daisy Heath last summer. Qamty's croon, the emotion on his face, reminded him of a love song, sung in an uninhibited manner Lashqat wished he dared in front of Mamaj. How perverse it was, how absurd, to address such endearments to Crazy Pox and Aunty Blast, as if they were his sweethearts. A worse perversity than to have a husband in a star, or wear women's ornaments with the beard of a man. Shamans were exceptional, Lashqat understood. But he could not reconcile Qamty's love songs, and his love-face, with these affliction spirits, even if they disowned their past and had been tamed.

True night. The fifteen men and women of the community squeezed into a tent with space for Qamty to dance over the sick man. They huddled against its skin skirts, like a mother's, limbs drawn in from the circle where Qamty tramped and banged his drum, and imitated the animal movements of his helper spirits. His voice gave their barks and bugles, grunts and screeches, as they went out to track the stranger spirit down.

The shaman in trance performed impossibilities. His polyvocal voice, his energy. His costume, a gown sewn with every conceivable cosmic invocation in metal, was heavy, but he whirled in the air as if he were the weight of a bird, as if the clashing metal were feathers. No matter how wild his dance, his feet, unnervingly near, swerved away from his audience's knees and elbows. In session, they took comfort in his bizarre attributes, for he stood between the spirits, who were monsters, and themselves.

All harmful spirits were a shaman's purview. All the ill and illness-causing, the evil in their lives. Placid ceremonies, the worship of land guardians and animal gods—by contrast to this night-time tent, serene and dignified—could be led by a knowledgeable elder or conducted by an ordinary person.

The shamans defended them from evil; from bodily ills and mental afflictions and misfortune; from curses, persecution; from plagues. Aunty Blast had been responsible for a plague in deer, the worst of times in grandmothers' memory. She had been converted into a shaman's spirit before Qamty was alive, by a great shaman Grandmother Pajai met once. Now, in one of their own summer tents, they heard her voice through the mouth of the journey-shaman Qamty, and had to trust him, and trust that her conversion stuck. As for the new spirit, who had killed Agyr-Anja's wife…

Qamty's helpers found the new spirit skulking not far off. They tried to talk to it. "Hello. Who are you? We don't know you." That was Crazy Pox, with his pops and hisses after words.

Aunty Blast had a croak and a cough from her old plague days. "Come and meet our shaman Qamty. He's our friend."

By their encouragement, the audience knew the stranger came.

"What do we call you? What can our shaman call you?"

"F-f-foreign wifffe."

A new voice quavered, frail and afraid.

Qamty leapt upright and spoke directly, in his human voice, to the spirit. "Oh Foreign Wife," he called, with that endearment croon again. "Oh Foreign Wife. Oh Foreign Wife." It was all he had. But listening furiously for sounds from the spirit, he started to insert an inflection, a snatch of tune: the beginnings of her song. The spirit's song, sung back to her by a shaman, pieced together out of her own disjointed phrases and stray words, from noises significant to her, that she used often.

In this way, shamans had learned songs for Crazy Pox and Aunty Blast. Clues to the spirit's biography, fragments, isolated images and short obsessive thoughts, jumbled up—

harsh, discordant, when judged by human song, with terrible things said in them. As long as the spirit felt the lyric true and responded.

"Oh Foreign Wife," Qamty sang as a first line of verse, with a soft urgency and a gentleness—as if she were his wife in frightful trouble, thought Lashqat, as if this were the woman he loved, violent and insane.

The spirit burst into visibility at the peak of the tent, beneath the smoke hole. People yelled—they had not been warned. Then they froze, pressed against the tent skirts, not to attract its attention.

It displayed itself as a goshawk with torn jesses on its legs and an exasperated glare in the eye.

Qamty immediately used this material. "Oh Foreign Wife, oh goshawk with torn jesses," he sang in a loud, glad voice to greet her, with glad gestures in his dance.

The goshawk seemed to gag on its own anger, with that maddened action you might see in an ill-trained hawk, mistreated, who had torn its leg-tethers loose to escape. Perhaps, thought Lashqat, the foreign wife knew such a hawk in her earthly life, to cast this symbol for herself. As understood through a hawk's body language, she had poked in for a look, and now thought to fly away again at any second. "But come and eat." Qamty grabbed a crescent moon of metal from his costume and cut into his arm. By shaman's art—for the metal moon was scarcely a functional knife—he sliced off the fleshy portion of his left arm below the elbow. This raw flesh he held up in his right hand.

The hawk seemed uncertain, jabbing its head forward, with that horrible gag in its throat. Qamty's mutilation might have been in vain.

Everyone murmured thankfulness when the goshawk flew downwards, perched on Qamty's upper arm, its talons in his gown, and took his offer of food. It ate quietly, and the audience kept as still as for a moment of trust from a real wild hawk.

Afterwards, Qamty let it fly away without interception, out of the too-small smokehole and out of visibility again. In its wake, Qamty collapsed.

He fell, and before Lashqat reached him, the sick man lifted on his elbows. He had been unconscious several days. He gazed around and slurred, "What's going on?"

Qamty lay on the floor-skins in a faint. However, there was no blood about him, and his left arm in its sleeve was found to be intact.

•

Next morning, the sick man continued to improve, while the shaman was exhausted. When he woke from the sleep that resembled a faint, his face had aged twenty years. They assumed that effect was temporary.

Even before the shaman rejoined them, the fifteen men and women of his audience had come up with a likely identity for the spirit they met in the night. "Yailaq had a foreign wife," they told him when he sat down with them, dull with fatigue. "From Aliangqot. She never settled in, and she drowned herself. They say her legs were caught in branches underwater when they tried to fish her up. We thought the leg rash might indicate her scratches, and of course the aversion to water."

"Why did she drown herself?" asked Pyrgy, the eldest girl, who had led the shaman's soft stags safely home. "Was she driven to it? Was he cruel?"

"Yailaq wasn't a cruel husband," said a grandmother who had known him, and the drowned wife, fifty years ago. "But timid. He didn't stand up for her when the main camp family had her run around like a servant and called her 'the Aliangq-ot' instead of her name. I was Pyrgy's age. And me? I've forgotten her name. I cannot tell you. But none of us forgot the sight of her, dragged out of the water."

"It was fifty years ago." This from the sick man's son, openly disgruntled. "I don't see what a dead woman's got to do with my father. She nearly killed him. Or Agyr-Anja's wife? She isn't descended from those families, no more than my dad. It's history."

The shaman, content to listen while they discussed her story, had to answer this challenge from the son. "Nothing is history to an ill spirit," he said mildly. "Unlike us, they don't forget, for they experience their human lives as a constant present. When a hurt animal lashes out, does it choose who to kick? Hurt and confused, with bad associations around 'that type of man' or 'a woman with that air.' A hurt animal defends itself and kicks the one who comes to help it. Shamans know."

"It isn't fair."

The tired shaman lost his temper for a moment. "If I had a bead for every time a client has said that to me, I'd be lit up like the spirits' festival lights in the sky."

As he spoke, he pointed to the pretty, treasured beads worn by the grandmother who had known the drowned woman. This they construed as a hint as to how he'd like to be paid. It was a question on their minds because first contact with an unknown spirit was dangerous work and ought to be paid well.

Patient again, with the remains of irritability on his face, Qamty nodded around the group. "You, the friends of the sick man, have to accept that a community similar to yours—that looks like yours to the spirit—failed her, and with its petty cruelties killed her by small cuts. I am not a convocation met to judge the matter. I don't deal in fairness," he directed to the son. "I do try to mend what harm has been done."

"Can you tame the spirit, shaman?" one asked him.

"Oh, it is a great work to heal a spirit. I have made a start. Other shamans can use the knowledge I have gained, and I too may have my chance with her again. I have cured your friend, I think—on the promise of that goat. Black-spotted," he reminded them. "White tuft in its tail."

Mention of the goat caused another little controversy. In scantily-clad complaint, the son told him, "I'll get her a spotted goat. We have to buy from the sheep and goats people, which means a trip, and once they hear you're after a specific kind of animal for sacrifice, they charge." His face scrunched up in speculation. "I don't see why a spirit is so fussy."

"A spirit has her reasons," Qamty said cheerily. "Maybe she suspects, if a sacrifice were too plain and easy, you'd forget about her again."

He left that day. Pyrgy imagined him with his soft stags and his husband in a star, not lonely at all. Lashqat saw him off with the tribute of a line from a tale. "The stitching Taliat said to Paliap perplexed, 'A shaman works in grief and love as I work in skin and sinew.'"

Before he was three miles from them, one of the community asked another, "That feat he did, do you think it was a trick? I bet he had animal meat up his sleeve."

Bryn Hammond writes the *Amgalant* series, historical fiction that is a close reading of the *Secret History of the Mongols*. Her *Voices from the Twelfth-Century Steppe* discusses her engagement as a creative writer with this primary source. She believes we often underestimate people of the past, and crude them down—her purpose is to battle this. Queer, poor, and cheery, Bryn lives in a coastal town in Australia, where she likes to write while walking in the sea.

Website: amgalant.com. Tweets: @Jakujin.

HANDBAG MEMORIES

by Lorraine Schein

My father told people he was a handbag designer, but he was actually a patternmaker. He had learned his trade in Europe the old-fashioned way, as an apprentice, before he came to America.

He had been in a work camp during the Holocaust and met my mother, also a survivor, here in New York.

My mother always joked that though she was married to a handbag designer, she never had a decent handbag. She didn't like the fancy ones he brought home for her.

He would go to the expensive New York department stores, like Saks Fifth Avenue and Lord & Taylor, and buy designer handbags to copy. He would take them home to our basement where he kept his cutting tools and study their construction. Then he would cut out patterns on the ping-pong table to make knock-offs of them for the handbag company he worked for to manufacture. Afterwards, he would return the bags to the store.

The salespeople got to know him well and were wary of him. Once, he had me return a bag he had bought to a store because he was afraid the saleslady would recognize him and not let him buy bags there anymore.

Like me during lockdown, my handbag has been nowhere in over a year. It still has the items it carried in March 2020—a few lip balms and lipsticks, wallet, keys, mini-notepad, my store discount cards, pens, Metrocard, emergency candy, my Chinese astrology glass animal good luck charms….

Now that I've been vaccinated, my handbag will soon be going back out with me into the world, though I'll stock it with a face mask and antibacterial wipes, precautionary hold-overs from my pandemic life. It will no longer be just a relic and wistful reminder of pre-COVID times.

Lorraine Schein is a New York writer. Her work has appeared in VICE *Terraform, Strange Horizons, Underland Arcana*, and *Mermaids Monthly*, and in the anthology *Tragedy Queens: Stories Inspired by Lana del Rey & Sylvia Plath. The Futurist's Mistress*, her poetry book, is available from Mayapple Press: www.mayapplepress.com

THAT DAY IN MY BEDROOM

by Karen Rollins

Our arms lay bare and parallel on the lavender quilt that sprawled across my springy twin-sized bed. Bubblegum swelled between our faces. Our shins lined flush on the hardwood floor, and our torsos pressed against the side of the mattress. We were mesmerized and intrigued by both the mirror image and the contrast of our bodies. I think we saw each other for the first time.

"Chocolate and vanilla!" I blurted out, lifting the spell.

"Sadie and Ginny!" Jessie followed up, in reference to her two different colored cats, and with that analogy, we giggled and gave each other high-fives, even before they were known as high-fives.

An abundance of bonding hormones filled the crevices of our tender hearts that beautiful Utah day in 1975. Dark green painted-looking trees dotted a wide dirt-colored mountain standing less than a mile behind my house. We were both ten years old and as gentle and carefree as its fresh canyon breeze easing through my window screen.

I had no better friend than Jessie, a girl who never met a Lip Smackers she could resist but could hold her own with me, a girl who would rather collect Topps baseball cards. Since the summer's beginning, we had rolled out of our respective beds into each other's presence. We often started the day canvassing our spacious subdivision on bikes, later abandoning them for the neighborhood playground and a fierce game of tetherball. Sometimes we would navigate through what we called "the fields," where vacant acres of sparse, stubbly grass and wildflowers, wiry shrubs, and the occasional tumbleweed covered powdery dirt. Various trails led to greener areas, where walkers hiked, campers roughed it, and lovers loved in secret, or so they thought.

Our curiosity spared no one, not even the local motorcycle gang. They met near large shady trees where the land was the greenest and hidden down a slight hill. Led Zeppelin and Neil Young roared from an outdoor hi-fi system, beckoning us to peek from behind the chest-high weeds and wild bushes to observe scenes that could have been *Woodstock* converged with *Easy Rider*. Long-haired dudes, hippie chicks, booze, marijuana smoke, leather, denim, laughter, motorcycle revving, cursing, and the smell of steaks on the portable grill kept us entertained until they didn't anymore. Eventually, boredom would lead us to the Circle K for Coke, Doritos, and a pack of Bubble Yum before rounding back to one of our homes to play with Barbies.

Despite the incredible amount of time together, before that day in my bedroom, we had never stopped to marvel at one another's differences. Seconds later, Jessie abruptly removed her arm from my bed, her eyes filled as if on the verge of crying. I held my breath and waited to learn if something embarrassing had occurred, like she'd wet her pants or lost a tooth—instead, she said nothing.

"What's wrong?" I asked.

Her voice trembled. "It's not fair."

"What's not fair?"

"I can't tell you." She stared at her fingers, pulling at them.

"Yes, you can. Please. What's not fair. Tell me."

She looked at me with her tear-coated blue eyes, and said, "That God made you Black and not white like me. It makes me so sad because you're so good." She did not sweep her light brown hair from her face as she lowered her head.

Internally, the humming began. *Jesus loves the little children. All the children of the world.* I slumped to the floor and stared at my hands resting in my lap. *Red, brown, yellow, black, and white.*

My brown skinned hands had never made *me* cry. They were the color of my mother's, my grandmother's, and my aunt's hands. Black hands who fed, bathed, and sheltered me from harm. My hands were the color of their love. My face was the color of Diana Ross's, the most glamorous woman I had ever seen, and my lips were the color of songstress Aretha Franklin's, who not only sang like an angel, but like a queen. Our collective features were reflected in the faces of the men and women covering every *Jet*, *Ebony*, *Essence*, and *Black Enterprise*. The magazines arrived monthly in our family's mailbox, and then appeared on my bedroom desk, courtesy of my mother, the magazine fairy.

Here I thought Jessie and I were celebrating our differences with equal appreciation—instead, we had unleashed her pity. The hum continued ever so forceful under my breath. *They are precious in his sight. Jesus loves the little children of the world.*

"It's okay, Jessie," I said. "I don't mind being Black. I like it." I watched tears plummet from her pink cheeks down to the tops of her white hands lying in her lap. In a strange way I felt special to know her tears, though not necessary, were shed over me. I put my arm around her shoulder and told her everything was going to be alright, the way I had learned to do when my younger brother cried.

We never spoke about that day afterward. Summer fun resumed and our focus moved to new places to explore and people to spy on. I've sometimes pondered whether Jessie's underlying emotion was born of empathy or a feeling of superiority. The adult me leans towards her compassion. In the five years of our friendship, I had witnessed numerous scenes move her to tears, from Disney characters in despair to roadkill on the side of the road. The likelihood that a ten-year-old possessed enough foresight to presume her best friend would face more challenges in life because of her skin color is astonishing, but plausible considering her sensitivity. I've also considered that the moment brought forth her awareness of white privilege, and the realization this benefit would never extend to me was what provoked those strong feelings of sorrow.

My skin color continues to arouse strong emotions in others. Though it has never evoked tears again, it often preconditions others' adverse views of my value, worth, integrity, and determination of what I deserve before those views can be proven wrong. The deaths of Sandra Bland and Breonna Taylor highlight what it means in terms of justice. If I didn't know my history and was not confident in this skin, I would have succumbed to all the subtle and blatant ways American society insinuates that Blackness is a flaw or a curse. Even implying this to children where it simmers in their minds and on occasion is expressed from their innocent mouths.

It's no surprise Jessie and I didn't stay best friends forever. Over a year later, when we started junior high, we had grown apart for reasons that may have had less to do with race than with becoming teenagers. We simply found new interests and new best friends. I was content to stay home Saturdays to read or bake pizza with like-minded friends, and she became more fashionable and a pro at figuring out which male admirer she would allow to take her to football games.

The *fields* seemed boundless back then, like they went on forever. Not only did they offer fresh air and a canyon breeze, they gifted unbridled freedom, acceptance, and equal footing for anyone who entered. But like all good things, in reality, they had their boundaries too.

In the summer, towering and smiling wildflowers bowed along the ends and sides of the farthest pathways, rows of them. There was even wonder as to whether *Oz* or a pot of gold existed on the other side. Sometimes when I hear songs like "Cinnamon Girl" by Neil Young or "Take it Easy" by the Eagles, I tap my feet, close my eyes, and think of those sunflowers. There are times I am even transported back to that day in my bedroom. Like now, I reminisce about the joy of having such a wonderful friendship with Jessie, someone with whom to share those memorable adventures. Then as quickly as the memories arrive, they depart, and what lingers is a touch of regret and sadness. For had we not stopped playing to compare our arms, maybe we would have continued to see ourselves as just children, instead of colors.

Karen Rollins dreams of the day when she can write all day, every day, near a body of water, preferably an ocean. In the meantime, she finds pleasure in writing inland at her desk in North Little Rock, AR, going on road trips, sightseeing, attending festivals of all kinds, and playing with her dog, Bucky. Her writing has appeared in *The Write Launch* and the anthology *(Her)oics: Women's Lived Experiences During the Coronavirus Pandemic*. Twitter: @pastwillow

SNOW SLED

by Deborah L. Bean

"**M**ommy, I tired—"

I looked down at my two-and-a-half-year-old daughter in her raspberry colored snowsuit. Her hood was up over her crown and falling over her forehead, with a thick scarf wrapped around her so many times that all you could see were her pale blue eyes and a strand or two of her white-blond hair. Through all the wrapping, her voice was muffled like the snow that surrounded us.

Near us, my four-year-old son was grabbing at the snow that towered on each side of the sidewalk of a quiet urban side street in Winnipeg, Manitoba. The banks loomed high over my head in many places. He would make snowballs with his mittened hands and, bouncing with excitement, would throw them at parked cars, street signs, even the fire hydrant. In this early evening walk towards home, it was well below freezing, especially since the sun had already set almost two hours ago. As usual, my feet were glacial in my cheap knee-high boots, my knees only protected from the cold by the pantyhose I wore. In those days we wore dresses to work. Thankfully, hemlines were no longer at mid-thigh that year.

"I know, sweetie, I'm tired too. But it's only two more blocks and we're home. You're my big girl, you can make it,"

I said, looking off into the distance towards home. Just two more blocks…

We'd left our apartment about twelve hours before, in the dark of the pre-dawn morning with just the slightest tinge of pale yellow light seeping above the horizon and the twinkling stars beginning to fade. Once again, the wind had drifted yesterday's heavy snow over the door of the building's entrance in the night. That made it impossible to exit my apartment through the front door.

Living on the second floor, I'd learned how to slide out of our living room window down to the ground on the snowdrift that always amassed up against the building's wall after snowstorms. It would be later in the day before the caretaker shoveled the walks.

I would slowly pull up the window pane, careful of the snow piled above the level of the sill to keep it from falling into the room. A couple of towels below on the floor kept the carpet dry. Bending double and stepping out, I'd pack the snow down a bit, cautiously so as not to fall. Then I'd help Davy out, followed by his sister, Shanna. Each of my children would slide down into the parking lot next to the building while I closed the window. My children thought the slide was fun and a terrific way to start the day. I was the only one who had to worry about snow up my butt. Then, we'd walk the four blocks to my first bus stop of the morning and wait, in the slowly lessening dark.

One morning, in the minus-forty frigidity, out of curiosity or some other precocity, my daughter had stuck out her tongue and frozen it to the metal frame of the bus shelter. Before I could stop her, she yanked her head away with a shriek. A straight line of taste buds from her tongue, like a string of pearls, was left on the structure—one tiny, glistening, frozen dot after the other. Luckily a wad of tissues was in my pocket as her mouth kept bleeding. Bus passengers had been helpful that day, pressing tissues on me, an offering of white bouquets springing from the hands of older, and wiser, heads. These fellow commuters were known to all three of us because we were daily riders on the same buses in a constant repetition of travelling to work and then back home, both mornings and evenings.

During the thirty-minute ride to another part of town, I usually conversed with my children, often spending quiet moments teaching them about the world and some of the things we saw. My son, with his blinding intelligence even at that tender age, was curious about everything, remembering and rattling off facts he learned. My daughter's own intelligence was more like street smarts. She could read people almost from the cradle, eagerly going to some but backing away from others in fear. From the time she could crawl, she'd always tried to get away from my ex. I often wished I'd had her advice before I got married, although I doubt I would have listened. Anxious to escape the man who was my father, I had accepted the first man who seemed so strong when I was seventeen.

After the first bus ride, my little ones and I would walk a block to the daycare located in the basement of a church. This was well before Mother's Day Out pre-schools showed up everywhere, so a daycare in a church was unusual. The staff there was well-trained and great with all of the kids, often sharing moments of their triumphs and tears with me at the end of each day. I received daycare for free because of their sliding scale based on income, but they never made me feel like a charity case. Their subsidy meant I was able to work full-time and teach my children that money didn't come in the mail.

Once inside the bright rooms of the church, where hot chocolate and oatmeal were waiting for them, I'd help my daughter get out of her winter clothes and put them in her assigned large tub. My son could do it himself, so that saved me a few minutes every morning. Each of their tubs contained a sweater, a change of clothes, and a small blanket and stuffed toy for naptimes. Davy's was a small blue cookie monster with googly eyes, and Shanna's a soft and well-loved velveteen rabbit.

If I was fast enough, I could catch the next bus headed downtown. If I was delayed, I waited another 20 minutes for the one following. Winnipeg at the corner of Portage and Main, was unarguably the coldest and windiest city intersection in the world. I spent many mornings huddled in the shadow of a skyscraper so I could switch buses, again hoping to time my transfers to reduce the minutes standing outside in the gusts and cold.

At the end of that third ride, I had the option of waiting for a fourth bus that would drop me off right in front of my workplace or hiking that last mile. I often opted for the walk just to keep warm. My feet would be frozen, my ears and nose numb, and my body would be wracked with the cold so far north of the southern Texas coast where I was raised.

If everything went right, I was at my desk before eight. In Canada, the sun was finally up by that hour. Until 4:00 pm, I worked at the Manitoba Hog Producers Marketing Board as an accounting clerk. My job was sorting the tickets that came off of the slaughtered hogs so that each farmer was paid correctly for the pigs he had sold at market. It was not a fun job. The tickets often came back covered in dried hog blood, fat, and other fluids, but it paid well enough that I could support my two darlings. My coworkers were generally supportive of me—the youngest of them all and a single mother.

"Mommy—can't! Carry me."

I could hear the tears in Shanna's voice that cold evening there on the sidewalk that had been turned into a white canyon of ice and snow. I looked at my bundled arms, my heavy purse and her backpack dangling from my hands. My son had his pack strapped across his shoulders as he took a karate chop at the snowbank to our side. Where Davy got his energy, I never knew, although come bedtime he could fall asleep harder than anyone.

"Kookamunga! Ha!" he shouted using his word of the month. No, it was almost a year that I listened to that word. Everything was kookamunga to him. I was still proud of him though, and his brilliance and actions brought a smile to my face. He was all wrapped up like his sister in his own dark blue snowsuit.

I had saved for months to be able to afford those suits, and I bought them two sizes too large so I'd get more than one year out of them. They kept my children warm as we trekked everywhere in the six-month-long winter, to places such as grocery stores, doctors, the bus stop, or the occasional six-block walk to McDonald's as a special treat. Their winter clothes were of far better quality than my own cloth coat.

"It's just a little farther, honey, you can make it," I cajoled, her hand in mine, hard to do wrapped in thick mittens. Bundled up in that fat and bulky snowsuit, I knew there was no way I could carry her.

I thought of the evening ahead. We'd get home around six, as usual. Once the kids were playing in the living room, I'd make supper. It was Tuesday, so I'd pull out a half-pound of frozen fish fillets. They came welded together in a box back in those days, and I always cut the box in half when I got home from the store so that the one pound box made two meals.

After peeling off the thin cardboard and paper wrapping, I'd put the block in a glass baking dish with a can of tomato soup, two sliced carrots, a finely chopped slice of onion, and a sliced celery stalk on top. It would bake for 25 minutes. During that time, a cup of salted water would come to a boil and I'd add a third of a cup of rice. Sometimes, I'd heat up a can of green beans if there was extra in the cabinet. Everything would be done at the same time. I'd become an expert on 30 minute meals—before microwaves.

We'd eat in the drafty dining room of our apartment at an old aluminum table and mismatched chairs. I couldn't afford a rug for the tile floor so it stayed cold. I always ate slowly in those early days of singlehood because if my son was still hungry, I'd give him some of my rice. He was growing so fast that I knew I'd have to adjust recipes soon, hopefully after next year's raise. When we were done, they would each get a slice of cheese. It was a big cheat on my part, convincing them that cheese was dessert.

After dinner, I'd bathe my daughter and then cuddle with her while her brother took his bath. Once he was done, we would read stories together for 20 or 30 minutes, or sometimes we would play a game or watch a little television if I felt it wasn't just garbage TV.

At eight o'clock, on the dot, it was time for bed. Once they were settled down after teeth-brushing, prayers, and a kiss, I then had time to clean house, get the kids' clothes and my lunch ready for the next day, and study for my Saturday computer class. After a bath, I would try to make it into bed by eleven, although it was often midnight. I had to be ready to start the next day at 4:45 in the morning.

"No!" said my daughter to my encouraging words. "I ti-red!"

Although she was too worn-out to actually do it, I could hear her stamp her foot in frustration in my head; she was quite good at getting her way with that move. Suddenly, she sat down in the middle of the sidewalk, *plop-shmoosh*, as her bottom and her bulky suit hit the ice. I didn't know what to do, I was so overwhelmed. Thousands of miles away was the warm sunny coast of Texas where I'd grown up.

I'd come to Winnipeg with my Canadian husband. It was far away from my troubles at home. My husband was now my ex, and he'd taken off over a year ago. We never received a penny from him. Between low-income housing, Canadian child allowance, my full-time job, and a part-time one on the weekends, we were still barely making ends meet. I was also taking a class or two every semester at the community college to try to increase my earning potential—but it was hard, not to mention exhausting. If not for the two in front of me, I would have given up long before. I had to be strong for them. I knew there were easier ways to make money—I'd been offered a few by men as controlling as my ex. The only reason I hadn't followed that path was to ensure the safety of my children. I got away from my ex before he started hitting them; I had to set an example for them. I was the only one to come away from his wrath with a broken nose and scars across my forehead.

And here was my daughter sitting in the middle of a freezing Canadian winter—because I couldn't even afford a car! They were calling it the worst winter in a hundred years. The temperature hadn't been above freezing in months. Most nights it fell to forty or fifty below zero!

I looked at my small, sweet daughter and wanted to join her, to throw a fit in the middle of the sidewalk at the unfairness of it all. How was I going to get her home? I was only twenty-two for God's sake!

My son, in typical big brother fashion, bounded over to her, "Shanna-nana! Up. Time to go home."

"No! Tired!"

She lay back flat on the ground. I watched as he tried to pick her up, to be a help to me. He felt his responsibility as the man of the house very strongly.

As he pushed and pulled at her, I noticed, with a *swish-swish*, that she was sliding around on her back over the slick snow and ice that had been trampled by many feet.

This year, with so much snow and cold, there'd been no chance for the drifts on each side to melt, so they'd just gotten taller and taller as people shoveled away just enough to break a passageway, throwing the snow up on top of the mounded verges. The towers' walls with their black, grey, and white streaks were banded like old black-and-white photos of the Grand Canyon, the dark and light layers of snow, smoke, car exhaust, and dirt separating each snowfall. Every so often, the cliffs were cut as a sidewalk led to other buildings, but our home was at the end of the street.

What I needed was a snow sled; then I could just pull her along. Again I saw her slide across the snow with her brother pushing at her. The movement made her giggle. Suddenly, a way to get home came to me.

"Sweetie, do you want to be a snow sled? Here, let me show you." I turned her around so her head was pointed in the direction of our apartment. "Tell me if this hurts. Okay, honey?" I said as I pulled on her hood and started dragging her across the icy sidewalk. The suit was slick and stiff in the cold and slid across packed snow. It would be difficult, but doable.

"Davy, you go first, okay?"

"Ha! I'm the leader!" my boy cried as he marched ahead. "Kookamunga! Follow me!"

It seemed to take forever, but we finally made those last two blocks. When we got to the parking lot, I stared with envy at all the cars parked and plugged in for the night. It would be another year before I could afford the luxury of my own car, a ten-year-old pale blue VW Super Beetle that Shanna named the "boatwagon."

While we were away, the caretaker had been out and the sidewalk leading up to the building door cleared. I'd only had to crawl up that snow slide to the window once in the past, thank goodness.

We stumbled up into the building and up the single flight of stairs to our apartment. It wasn't much, but it was ours. We were safe and warm inside those doors with its used furniture, scrounged and found from wherever I could, much of it free from dumpsters. I turned up the heat in the apartment, and we started to warm up as we peeled ourselves out of our snow gear.

While I was making supper, my children played and Davy teased his little sister, "Shanna-banana's a snow sled! That's so kookamunga!" Now that my girl was home, she was suddenly less tired and ready to go for our nightly rituals.

I smiled at my children and like the rays of the sun bursting from behind dark clouds, my spirits were brightened. We were poor, but we were our own happy little family. I was working hard to provide for our future, and to see them carefree, protected, and cheerful, made this moment another joyous beginning to a too short evening.

And just think, tomorrow we would do it all over again.

Deborah Bean, a native Texan raised during the height of the moon race, became interested in science-fiction at a young age. A single mother at twenty, who struggled raising two children while attending college and working two jobs to better the lives of her children, in 2016, she completed the Your Novel Year Graduate Certificate at ASU's Piper Center for Creative Writing.

Her story, "Money Doesn't Come in the Mail," was published in *Story Circle Journal*, September 2014. She won First Place from the Writers Guild of Texas for "The Visiting Professor" in 2016. In 2019, Ms. Bean received a 3rd Quarter Honorable Mention from Writers of the Future for "Demons Out There." She was published in the 2019 and 2020 anthologies, *Real Women Write*, for "Why I Didn't Become a Young Writer" and "COVID and I are Getting Old in Dallas."

She currently lives in Dallas, Texas, with her husband, Neal Berkowitz, and two dogs.

THE SIGNATURE

by Vandana Nair

There is bittersweet regret when I sign my name. On bank forms, applications, credit card slips, and all official documents. My handwriting goes into turmoil as the stylus scrapes on the tablet. The script winking on the screen is mine, but the effort feels false. I appreciate the sense of relief when it's done, let go of the plastic pen as soon as I can, and flex my fingers a few times to free them of the numbness. For though the act of signing my proof of identity cannot be separated from a lingering feeling of remorse, my story is not about my own skill or literateness but about Anita, Sita, and Gita.

I was seventeen years old that summer of 1985 when I focused my attention on the three girls. My first public examination at the end of grade 10 was behind me, and I was nearing the end of high school. Self-reflection had become second nature as I toggled between Literature, Botany, and Social Sciences. My mother was hoping I would go to medical school, but I found flowers and trees more fascinating than dissecting Asian bullfrogs. Summer had been spent reading female idols like Sarojini Naidu and Ismat Chughtai, and to say I felt like setting the world on fire would be an understatement. India was still recovering from the brutal assassination of Indira Gandhi, our first woman Prime Minister. Her death had impacted me more than I could admit, and if it were left to me, I would have changed my name to Priyadarshini after the late Prime Minister, but I consoled myself by sacrificing my long tresses and replacing them with her trademark bouncy bob. If my classmates thought that my haircut made me look like a scarecrow, they never said it aloud, but I read their thoughts in their hung jaws and raised eyebrows. It also earned me the ire of my grandmother, who already fretted over my tiny button nose and "no looks to speak of." However, at that moment, I felt immensely liberated. I had decided that I wanted to be known for my work and not my looks. Following in the footsteps of my idols, I had to do my bit, perhaps start small, but trigger some social reform that would make a lasting difference.

My mother had taught me about gardens. She had always been my inspiration and was the one responsible for sowing the seeds of feminism in me. She had perfected the science of cultivating life, after losing my father at age 26. Having loved deeply, she had never remarried, choosing to return to her parents' home to bring up my brother and me on her own. Her younger sister, my aunt, was in a similar situation, with two daughters to raise and a husband lost to illness. In an unprecedented move, these two pragmatic women had chosen to combine their two households. We were four kids and four adults joined together by crisis—my mother took care of the house and kids, my aunt handled the family business of auto parts, and my grandparents were happy to provide a roof over our heads. While it may not have been emancipation in the most real sense of the word, for us, the four kids in the house, the unorthodox household gave us the freedom to explore new ideas and choices.

Unorthodox and large it was: the household. We were privileged to be part of that select group of people in India those days who were fortunate enough to own a black-and-white television. Besides watching TV, our chores mostly consisted of keeping ourselves clean, well fed, and academically inclined. A washerwoman would come and do laundry by hand, a skull-capped, Urdu-speaking man picked up our clothes for ironing, and a cleaning lady would come in to do the dishes and mopping. The cleaning lady would saunter in twice a day, three daughters in tow. Aged 15, 13, and 11, they dragged their feet after their mother, unwilling participants in work they had inherited by virtue of their birth. I watched this motley band of girls trail after their mother and help the poor woman pick up after us, chores that we could undoubtedly have managed had we not been so spoilt. But that summer in the eighties, I saw them, really saw them for the first time.

Anita, Sita, and Gita were like blossoms in appearance, body language, and expression. They wore fuschia frocks paired with dark green leaf-like ribbons in well-oiled pigtails, ponytails, and braids. They matched a bright colour with an even brighter shade as if to add cheer to their banal existence. Like graceful creepers dangling from branches, shiny bangles flashed on their wrists and colourful glass beads from their necks when they tried to embellish our pastel hand-me-downs with their own attempts at fashion.

Anita, the eldest, was like a bluebell, with the shy aura of a girl who had passed her childhood receiving grateful crumbs of affection. Her dusky complexion, sharp nose, and serious demeanour made her appear older than her 15 years until she smiled. Her gap-toothed smile, as rare as bluebells were to Asia, emphasised her cleft chin and transformed her face into a thing of unblemished beauty. Mostly, she looked humble and bowed down, as if the weight of the world was on her shoulders. It was up to her to ensure that her sisters behaved well and did their chores correctly.

Thirteen-year-old Sita was the middle child. Bashful like the peony, she was homegrown and wild. Like a woody shrub, she basked in long hours of sunlight. Her hair ribbons were ever askew, and multiple strands covered her eyes and face, which she brushed off at careless intervals when they fell too heavily upon her eyes. Her blooming period was always short. In the morning shift, she would be scrubbed pink and clean from head to toe, but by the time I clapped my eyes on her in the evening shift, she looked browner than brown, with patches of mud caked on her nose, chin, elbows, and the soles of her feet. A permanently parched look in her close-set, tiny eyes added to her unkempt appearance. She was short on style, and always on the lookout for something to eat, ensuring that her food portion was equal to Gita's. She probably hated the fact that Gita had usurped her place as the baby of the family.

That Gita was not related to her sisters by birth was apparent in her tall stature and big, dark-brown eyes. Her cheekbones, small nose, small chin, and small lips rested like small florets in a honey gold face. Like a young sunflower head, Gita exhibited heliotropism. She beamed towards the sun and charmed everyone around her, and I could see why it had been easy for her to settle into a new family. Her smile didn't say that her parents were dead. Maybe she believed they would appear one day to pick her up from this extended family stay. Maybe she loved being part of this mismatched flowerhood. Or maybe she was just happier here because she was being fed and nurtured. Whatever coping mechanism she used was fruitful because she did look the most joyous of the three.

The girls followed their mother to our home twice a day, morning and evening. They bobbed their heads and spoke in a dialect that was a mix of Hindi and their native vernacular Bhojpuri. Sometimes they imitated the four of us by tossing off English expletives like "shit," "idiot," and "stupid." When I met them on their evening shift on weekdays, they looked quite animated as Amma allowed them to watch TV with us. Sometimes they were disappointed, as the broadcast would be in English, and they would just stare at alien images of golden looking people whose lives looked far more glamorous than their own. One evening, I started translating *I Love Lucy* for them in Hindi. My literal translation of the encounter between Lucy and Mr Mooney became the leading entertainment of the evening and sprouted the idea of helping them learn English. I first broached the idea to my brother and cousins.

"Kaala akshar bhains baraabar, Chhoti," said my brother. He looked skeptically at me as if trying to make me understand the impossibility of my mission. For him, as in the Hindi proverb, black alphabet and buffalo were identical for an illiterate.

"They are like flowers," was all I said.

"Teach them four-letter words first," said my playful cousin. She was nearer to my age and could be an agent provocateur any time I attempted anything new.

"Can I be in your class, didi?" was the adoring response of my baby cousin. She seemed to be the only one open to the idea but too young to be of real help.

"You need to get their mother on board," advised my mother. "I know Mangala. Had they really wanted to learn, she would have done her best to admit them to a municipal school, beta."

Usually, when Amma called me "little one" in that tone, I knew she was trying to balance my expectations with a dash of practicality.

"Don't sit with your head close to theirs, they have lice…" whispered my class-conscious grandmother.

"You can do it, but they don't have money to spend on books, my chidiya," added my gentle grandfather, trying to spare my feelings.

His slight encouragement was all that I needed. I was his little bird, destined to fly. My resolve firmed up. Besides, losing our Prime Minister had woken the sleeping crusader inside me—I felt I had to at least give it a try.

I remember anxiously waiting for the girls to appear for their evening shift. As soon as they did, I cornered their mother in the kitchen. If the girls were like flowers, Mangala, their mother, was the prickly pear cactus. A short, stubby woman with a dauntless air, she looked and behaved like a survivor who could take on wet summers and cold winters and still stand. Unlike my Amma, who always smelled mildly of lemons, she reeked of pungent odours like garlic, spices, and mustard oil intermingled with the sour smell of squalor. A threadbare sari, faded from too many washes, wrapped her stout frame, and only her pockmarked face betrayed a small residue of colour for she took genuine pains to prettify it. Besides a ginormous red vermilion pad-like dot on her forehead, she wore a heavy gold nose-pin and lined her eyes with thick, black kohl that made her features look pinched and pointed in contrast. Her teeth gleamed as bright as the oil in her hair that she tidily parted mid-way and twisted into a tight bun at her nape. I could see that my request had temporarily replaced her usual air of defiance with that of astonishment.

"Study? Why English, baby? All they need to know is cooking and cleaning like me," she said.

"If they know how to read and write, they will get better work later. In an office! Don't you want that?" I said.

"But baby, how will they go to the office? Who will give them work? You don't know how lazy they are…" She sighed and gave me a piercing look. Mangala hated laziness. She probably thought we were lazier than her three daughters and that I could possibly do something better with my time like keeping my room in order.

"Don't you want them to at least sign their name?" I prodded. "Do you like it when they put their thumbprint on the ration card?" The ration card, a government-issued card for buying cheaper groceries and provisions for every registered Indian family, was a document akin to a passport.

"But they need to help me morning and evening," she snapped. "Where do they have the time?" That she was feeling tetchy was apparent when she started twisting the free end of her sari around her index finger. The faded block print caught my eye, and I recognized it as one of Amma's old saris.

"What about afternoons?" I offered. "Isn't that their free time? Right after I am back from school, I can sit with them for an hour."

"Alright baby, but just for an hour, and only because they are coming to your house. But how do I pay for the lessons?" she challenged.

"Don't worry about the fee or books. The day they sign their name, I will know that I have received my fee." I left the kitchen before she could change her mind.

•

I remember walking around in a state of bliss the entire day and burning my pocket money on basic English and Hindi primers, three notebooks, and pencils. Amma had yielded a small corner in the courtyard for the lesson. The courtyard lay between the dining room and the bedrooms and was hardly private. A screen mesh door opened into the kitchen to give their mother a diagonal view of the class, but budding crusaders could not be choosers. Whether the strategic location had been my mother's idea or Mangala's was debatable, for both had vested interests. I had covered the ground with a mosaic-print, tribal black and red rug from my room, and put three small footstools atop it, which would work as makeshift desks. Primers, notebooks, pencils, and scented erasers lay on each stool. A slate, duster, and chalk rested on a table next to my chair. Being the teacher, my chair was slightly higher than their sitting arrangement, and I hugged the elevated status warm within my soul. It was a patched-up classroom at best, but the effort had generated a feeling of anticipation like I finally had the purpose for which I had been searching. Finally, the three girls arrived on the planned afternoon.

I looked at them with great optimism, for they had taken pains with their appearance. For a change, they looked quite similar, with hair neatly combed and braids freshly done. Even Sita's face had been scrubbed clean. Their matching yellow frocks were an unlikely uniform, but to me, the gesture spoke of effort—like they were as excited to learn as I was to teach.

"Do you know why you should learn to read and write?" I said.

"So I can marry English boy," giggled Anita shyly.

"Didi, I can see English TV," said Sita in her Pidgin English.

"You mean you can marry a boy who speaks English, and you can watch English programs on TV," I corrected them carefully, trying not to laugh.

"What about you, Gita?" I turned my attention to the youngest.

"I want to be Hema Halini," she spoke clearly in Hindi.

I was taken aback. I knew Gita was referring to the famous Indian actress and danseuse, Hema Malini, who carried the moniker of Dream Girl from one of her films. Her words exposed healthy ambitions to rival mine, and I knew this class could be a stepping-stone towards her dreams.

"You mean Hema *M*alini?" I stressed the M sound so she could pronounce the name correctly. "Why?"

"Because I look like her," she preened.

Sita pulled her braid hard.

"You look like a monkey," she said, and both older sisters started laughing delightedly at her.

"Stop," I frowned at them. "Of course Gita can become a star if she wants to," I said. I relaxed my face into a smile and told myself that if I was hoping to be successful at social reform, I absolutely could not afford to have favourites.

"And so can both of you!" I added. I turned and looked straight into Gita's eyes.

"As a big star, you will earn a lot of money Gita, and if you don't know how to read or write, people will cheat you."

Her eyes rounded at the mention of money and were twinkling at the prospect of becoming a big star. She picked up her scented eraser and sniffed long and loud into it. I could see that she was already in a rosy-pink daydream.

"You teach makeup, didi?" she piped up, elated at my unvarnished support but clearly thinking of bigger things.

I stared at the three eager faces. They looked excitedly back at me. This was not how it was supposed to be. The girls were supposed to jump at the chance of being educated, and not barter for something else. I looked at the books and stationery I had squandered half of my monthly allowance on and wondered why they wanted makeup. The tips of my ears reddened, and I could hear peals of laughter emanating from the dining room. I knew without a doubt that my brother and cousins had their ears trained on the lesson, and I gathered my crumbling patience, hoping against hope that this was just the "getting to know each other" phase. I was sure things would improve once we got into the flow of the class. Like a new mother trying to shush her child out of a tantrum, I resorted to the only option open to me.

"If you study hard, I will teach you how to use makeup, but first open your copies!"

And so the flowers began their lessons. Whoever said that the road to hell was paved with good intentions, was probably right. Our second lesson didn't go any better than the first. After several misunderstandings and unsatisfactory conclusions, the lessons went on for a couple of months. On certain trying days, I wished I never had to see them again in my life. Then one of them would say "sorry" in their guilt-ridden, lilting tone, and my enthusiasm would return with a vengeance. What I do remember clearly is my heady anticipation of the lessons, as I slowly cycled, counting trees on my usual route back from school. My bicycle would first cross mango and maulshree trees along Dilkusha Road, followed by the golden-yellow flowers with silver and green leaves of the kanak champa near the Command Hospital, and then the shocking pink of the tabebuia on the last stretch. The bright hues would remind me of the girls, and I would pedal faster.

The excitement of teaching them, the wolfing down of lunch and milk in expectation of their arrival, remains forever etched in my mind and heart. I remember trying hard to teach them how important it was for them as young women to be literate, to bloom into their potential and to write their own destinies, dressing up my garden-variety philosophy with symbols like food, songs, television, films, and images they found infinitely more relatable. At some point, I might have stumbled upon the realization that they would need to know the Hindi alphabet too, for it was their native tongue and they fell naturally back to it to discuss the images of "apple," "bat," and "cat" from the primer. They were rather snobbish about learning "only" English and puckered up their noses at the vernacular Hindi script, but I could not really blame them, for I felt I was doing the same. That long-ago summer, I was part of a wishful nation that seemed to have lost its distrust of its colonial occupiers. In retrospect, it makes me question my adolescent adulation of the late Prime Minister too. Had I been inspired by her elegant styling or her letter-perfect English speeches? Later in life, I did get over my blind hero-worship of Mrs Gandhi as I learned more about the crimes of the Emergency and questioned her dictatorial ways. Perhaps, growing up is just that, a slow pendulum process of swinging between all things black and white, until you pace yourself to a central, mid-way, mid-gray position. Gradually, I became more accepting of the regular blending of Indian languages with the rigidness of the Queen's English too, as I started studying in Mumbai and inhaled the vibrant polyglot street lingo of India.

This is how I remember those days. But I also remember the frustration of not being able to get my point across—of trying to sow seeds in a patch of wilderness. While we conversed in the girls' native tongue, Hindi, for clarity, the rules of engagement for the lessons, clearly defined by them, remained purely English. They were puzzled by the pronunciation. Based on "no" and "go" they said "do" and "to" with a long "o" sound and chortled at the "u" sound. They often resorted to Hindi and added "-ing" to every word, awarding it their own Anglicized status. At other times, when I tried to teach them the Hindi word so they could connect it with its English counterpart, they put their pencils and heads down in a woeful grimace.

"S-I-T-A," I said, spelling the letters in Sita's name as slowly as I could, and she wrote "S-I-T" and forgot the "a."

"SIT is to take a seat…" I stood and sat back on the chair to demonstrate the verb, and the other two rolled on the rug at Sita's apparent befuddlement at her mistake.

Not sure how to explain the "a" phonetic sound to Sita, I assumed that she would understand it better with the Hindi alphabet, and drew a picture of a mango. The Hindi word for mango or aam is one of the first fruits Indians learn as toddlers, so I asked Sita what it was in her native tongue, assuming that she would jump at my clue and grab it gleefully.

"Aam," she said and also added, "I am hungry. Can I have something to eat?"

"Hmmm…"

Mangala snorted aloud from where she stood hunched over the kitchen sink, scrubbing dishes from our lunch and glaring at the class that to her was a Sisyphean endeavour. Frustrated at their mulishness, I went back to the English alphabet.

•

Some afternoons I waited and waited, and by early evening Mangala would saunter in and say, "They are not coming…"

"Why?" I'd say, at the risk of getting my head bitten off.

"Stomachache," she would say. "Maybe I need to give them water for dinner tonight."

Standing before me, Mangala would gnash her teeth. Her eyes would glint in anticipation of the punishment she was going to inflict later. She would take the broom and start sweeping, every swipe at the floor almost an exaggerated gesture of disapproval. With a twisted smile, she would tell me that it was their ploy for avoiding work. She used these occasions to say that she had told me so.

I often wondered how the lessons had impacted Mangala's life. In my blind quest for altruism, had I made it harder for her? Had the class become an easy excuse for the girls to escape their chores? Would it really lead to a better life for her daughters? I hoped so and wished that they would arrive on time the next day. And sure enough, they did, on the promise of candy or nail paint or a new Hindi show.

The girls conveniently forgot their preference for English whenever a Hindi movie was playing on television on Sunday evenings. On Wednesday evenings, there was a show that featured Hindi film songs called *Chhayageet*, and sure enough, they would appear on the dot. They preferred clean-shaven, tall, fair Indian film heroes, and if the telecast featured the Kapoor brothers, who were trending in the eighties, they smiled coyly at each other and became acutely absorbed in the romantic numbers. If it was a Hema Malini song, Gita artlessly copied her dance moves until my brother's disdainful laughter would put her back in her place.

As I look back, I feel sheepish at my smug, younger self's dedication to the written word, while my wayward students clearly preferred brighter content that dressed up, moved, and sang to them. Friday nights were an anomaly, for they lingered in front of the television, just as we did, for the much-awaited telecast of *The World This Week*, albeit for different reasons. For me, the news magazine was my window to the bigger world, and it helped that the young and debonair Prannoy Roy hosted it. His neat black beard and British-inflected voice were a huge novelty because until then we had associated facial hair only with Bollywood baddies or decrepit Urdu poets. The girls thought him too old, for "beard" meant old men to them. Mostly they lingered for the latest music videos that were aired from the Eurotops lists right before the news magazine broadcast. Their eyes widened and their imaginations stretched at the sight of the skimpy, shiny outfits, multi-hued hair, and fluorescent eye shadow of the pop stars and what they interpreted as "gibberish" in English. As the theme music and graphics ended, the news magazine began, and they left at the sight of the bearded guy.

I remember their thrill the first time they saw Michael Jackson's "Bad" when it aired on a Friday night.

"Didi, this guy should use talcum powder…" Anita said that night as we watched MJ croon "Man in the Mirror" into the mic.

"What do you mean?"

"He looks brown like us…" was Anita's naïve observation.

"No golden hair…" said Sita.

"No shiny clothes…" said Gita, finding MJ's black jeans and white shirt too unglamorous for her tastes.

That evening was spent translating the larger macro of the song. I had gently rebuked Anita for her unfair comment on MJ's skin. The girls had listened to my racial harmony discourse with half an ear, maybe thinking that I was making much ado about "brown," and that most of the world's problems could be solved through makeup. As victims of their share of social inequality, they didn't really think much of the emaciated singers in the music videos and felt that rich, glamorous pop stars had no right to be in a less than perfect state.

"I am brown, Hema Halini is white, didi…" said Gita after giving it some thought, "because she has perfumed soaps…"

"Yes," said Anita. "He should use perfumed soaps." She beamed with pride at Gita.

I realized that it made a weird kind of sense to them and didn't have the heart to tell Gita that her beloved actress was not exactly white.

Not all shows needed translation, though. There was a Hindi show called *Udaan*, meaning "flight," that traced the life trajectory of the young daughter of a farmer who fought for her right to gain a more "respectable" position in society. Her fight for her farmer father, who had unjustly lost his land, appealed to the reformer in me. Inspired by the true story of India's first female Director General of Police, the show signified everything I wanted to do in my own life—battle gender discrimination and other conflicts before finding my road to success. However, the girls thought that the protagonist deserved better than the muddy green police uniform and the bearded guy in the end. I was shattered by their analysis.

"Why?" I said.

"She is pretty…" they cried in unison.

Later, I overheard them telling Mangala that I liked old, bearded men, and in a fit of annoyance, I asked Amma to restrict them from watching any TV besides Sunday movies.

•

All too soon, my own life took over. I had to choose my college majors at the end of the year, and as my mother never failed to remind me, that time leading to my final board examination was precious. Coupled with the challenges that I faced at school, I started doubting my own ability to teach. I especially remember a particularly traumatic debate at school. That afternoon, I cycled back home in a daze, oblivious of the trees, the flowers, and the roads. For the first time, I was unsure of where I was headed.

"How did the debate go?" Amma said, half-reclined on her pillow, her glasses resting on the book she had been reading.

My mother was a plump woman, who enjoyed her afternoon naps. Those days, when I came home from school, I often found her asleep. Sometimes she forced herself to keep reading until I got back. I loved that about her. Steady as an oak, her strength lies in the way she looks at things and tries hard not to pass judgment. Through the years, her long black hair has turned to a short crop of silver, her stoutness somewhat reduced, but her reading, her glasses, and her perspectives have stayed the same. That afternoon, though, I wished that she had not waited up. There was no escaping her, so I slowly sat down at the foot of the bed.

"I messed up…" And the dam of tears I had been saving up broke loose, its flow free and unrestrained. "The judge commented on my pronunciation twice," I gulped back more tears, "on the mic, in front of everyone."

"Maybe she wanted all the kids to learn and say the words correctly." Amma rubbed my back slowly, waiting for the tide of emotions to subside.

It hurt not only because our team had lost but also because the presiding panel of judges had been outsiders. One of them had corrected the way I said "hero" and "cacophony" at the end of the event. I had felt all eyes in the auditorium boring into me.

"Did you cycle back alone?" Amma asked.

"Yes. I didn't want to speak to anyone."

Usually, I cycled to and from school with two friends who lived down the road. But everyone had been too busy congratulating the winners. No one had bothered to come and speak to me or check if I was ok.

"I just wanted to come home," I said, wiping my face with the loose end of her sari.

"You will be better prepared next time," she said with finality.

Amma knew her seventeen-year-old too well. Adept at handling the three teenagers under her roof, she knew that the only drama I could ever abide was the one executed by my own self.

"Eat something now, your pigheaded class will be here soon."

In my anguish, I had completely forgotten about the girls. That moment, self-doubt raised its head. Whether digging this patch of land was even worth it in the bigger scheme of things. Whether I needed to think of my own future before helping others. However, in the next moment, just as a dog struts its high, stiff tail with a wagging tip, my fervour returned, alert and aroused. I took a silent vow to check the dictionary for the correct enunciation, to ensure that I did right by the girls when they moved to bigger and better words, and waited for my gaggle of little women, hoping that indulging in superior efforts would take the misery out of my day.

It did. That evening went by better than I had expected. For the first time, Anita wrote her name in English. At my cajoling, she also tried to write her name in Hindi, though she messed up the vowel signs. Sita had elbowed her sister in the ribs and induced some giggles. Was it my imagination, or had there had been a certain glow on Anita's usually sombre face that evening? Their playfulness had helped me put my own failure in perspective. I remember feeling that the time I had spent tutoring them had been well worth it.

The lesson had ended with my giving Sita and Gita homework to practice writing their names.

"Tomorrow, each of you will write your name, without looking at the notebook. Next time you take your provisions on the ration card, write your name. Don't use your thumb on the ink-pad."

•

My minuscule success had been celebrated that evening. I talked incessantly of my plans for the girls at dinner, and if my family thought I was rushing my expectations regarding their learning, they didn't mention it. I was sure that some ice had been broken, and from that day onwards, the girls would come of their own accord, now that one of them had tasted success. So I waited rather impatiently for the next three afternoons in a row, but there was no sign of them. Finally, at the risk of being told to concentrate on my own education, I checked with Amma regarding their whereabouts. She told me that the girls and their mother had gone to their native village.

"Why now? Just when I was making headway." I allowed my disappointment to show.

"Maybe it's time you focused on your own work, beta," she said.

"You know I am. I have started looking at undergraduate programs here. I have even looked at the application forms and circled the due dates for submission."

"Why only here? In Lucknow? Why not look at Delhi University too?"

That took me by surprise, the fact that my mother was comfortable with me leaving home.

"Guess I never thought of leaving you…" I said.

"Why not? Don't feel that you can't. I'll say the same thing I say to your brother. You can, if that's what you want to do!"

I felt the conversation slipping out of my hands.

"But what about the girls?" I wailed.

Just when I expected further reproof, my mother turned to me with her long-lived eyes.

"You know that you can only teach them if they want to learn, right?"

"But they are learning a bit, aren't they?"

From her carriage and tone, I knew that there was a life lesson coming my way.

"A little knowledge is a dangerous thing."

That day, I might have thought that she was referring to the girls. Now, I wonder if that nugget had been for me. Maybe my mother could see that Anita and I, both, were at the brink of discovering that we were not quite the experts we thought we were.

I single-mindedly pursued my mother for more information and she relented.

"They have all gone to their village. It seems there is a good marriage proposal for the eldest girl. If all works out, they want to get her engaged and married in the winter." She had busied herself with tidying the room around her, unwilling to make eye contact.

"Anita? But she is only 15…" I protested. "Didn't you tell them it's wrong for her to marry so young?"

"You think I didn't? The man is old enough to be her father…"

She continued to fold the clothes lying on the bed, but her mind was elsewhere. Her face was a composed mask—only her hands betrayed her agitation. Whether she was thinking of the next chore that she had to handle because of Mangala's absence, or figuring out the best way to tell me that she had cautioned Anita's mother against marrying her to a much older man, I knew I had touched a raw nerve. Amma, with her more substantial experience of the world, knew that sometimes in households like Mangala's, economics took precedence over righteousness. Unsure of my reaction, she was trying her best to remind me of my own priorities. I hated to see my mother, who was always ready with a solution for the trickiest situation, reach that impasse. Something pushed me into absolving her from giving me a clear answer.

"Can I help you with the chores?" I asked.

And we sat in silence and folded clothes together.

•

In the days that followed, I felt lonely, at home and at school. I did not wait for friends or conversations. The sun felt like a hot ball of fire blistering my back. All I noticed were the street dogs dozing off in the shade of the trees that stood like sentries on the never-ending, burning, grey asphalt roads that led home. I viewed the flowers, the trees, and the familiar roads with detached sorrow. Child marriages happened only in villages, I kept telling myself, and not in cities the size of my hometown, definitely not in this day and age. Perhaps this was why in an agricultural country like India, farmers looked for alternate occupations. Because they faced one failed crop after the other, the only options open to them were to marry off their young daughters or lose their land. Perhaps daughters who could chart their own destiny were found only on television. Realization slowly dawned that I had been focused on the right alphabet, the right pronunciation, when I ought to have pushed harder for the right tenet.

Slowly the idea of leaving my hometown grew. Home no longer seemed green, or organic, or safe, but shallow and regressive. It was a place without concern for the future of a fifteen-year-old girl. Even though I was unsure about leaving home, I thought about my ability to adapt to a new environment. I also wondered whether Anita would adapt to a new life or a new forty-two-year-old husband. I knew from science class that birds and bees could live on nectar produced by flowering trees, and many of the species I passed on my ride back could easily adapt to higher temperatures. Sometimes I wished human beings were more like flowering trees, ready to adapt anywhere and everywhere at the mere promise of food, sunlight, and water. Wasn't that why Mangala was prepared to marry Anita to a man old enough to be her father, for the promise of food, shelter, and water? In this way, what my mother had wanted all along finally happened, and I started looking at undergraduate schools in New Delhi and Mumbai.

One sultry afternoon, after two weeks of absence, just as I was sitting in my teacher's chair perusing forms for the School of Humanities in Delhi, Mangala turned up with her three daughters in tow. They had a definite air of satisfaction about them that I could not penetrate. The girls showed off their shiny, new nail paint. I looked at the purple-black ink stains on their thumbs, the ugly stains taking over where the shiny nail paint ended. The girls promised they would come back for a lesson the next day as they had really missed them. I knew it was their way of offering an olive branch and without further misgiving, I took it.

"Are you ok?" I asked Anita.

She smiled and looked back at me with newly acquired poise.

"Yes, didi. Do I need to come for the lesson tomorrow?"

"What do you mean?"

"My mother said I ought to pay attention to household work now," she said.

"Are you sure you want to get married?" I said.

"I am, didi. I will have my own house now."

"Have you met the guy?"

"Yes." She gestured at her chin and stroked it in an impersonation of a long beard. Whether she wanted me to know that I would like him or say that he was old is anyone's guess. She looked down at her feet, just then. Admiring her bright red toes, drooped like a bluebell. My composure slipped. Anita seemed oblivious to the injustice of her situation.

"You hate beards!" I cried out. "You can study, you can work, you can do so much with your life. You are only fifteen…"

She slowly raised her head and looked straight into my troubled eyes.

"The groom said I am beautiful. His family also liked me. I don't need to study or work."

My cheeks stung like I had been slapped hard. That's how hot they felt. I remember my eyes brimming with tears, as I looked down at my forms. I picked them up so that I could go to the privacy of my room, to weep. While I had been dissecting the girls for my social experiment, it had never crossed my mind that they were observing me, too. I still wonder if that was how the girls had seen me that long-ago summer? A skinny girl with a snub nose, a weird hairdo, and just a little less brown than themselves, so she had to study and work to add to her zero marital prospects.

The next day had been tortuous. My head felt heavy after a restless night spent tossing and turning. My day at school had passed in a blur. Sita and Gita arrived earlier than usual that afternoon. Their energy was infectious, and I found myself listening to their excited chatter. They had left Anita moping at home. It seemed that Anita's marriage could not take place until she was eighteen, so the groom's family was coming over the next day to talk about it. A weight lifted from my heart. It was like the Gods had heard my silent plea. Chiding myself for being impatient and losing hope too soon, I found myself open to compromise. As long as the family waited for Anita to turn eighteen, all would be right with my world. Heart back in the lesson, I taught my leftover protégés with renewed care. When Sita and Gita inscribed their names in their four-lined copies without a single mistake, I clapped for them and felt quite accomplished.

The next lesson could not come soon enough for me. Faith restored in the way my world had flooded with sunshine and other forms of life, I attacked my college applications with great vigour. Although I was not ready to choose between an education in Science or Humanities, I knew that eventually, I would figure it out. The very next day, on my way back from school, I gathered some golden-yellow kanak champas that had fallen on the ground, unable to withstand the force of the wind. For my bright gaggle of girls. I wanted them to feel the essence of their achievement. I also hoped to send off the completed Delhi University applications that day, in the spirit of attaining my own goals. Once home, I took special care to arrange the flowers into a bouquet.

Lunch finished, I was browsing the application forms for a final check. Only my signature at the end of each form remained. The girls had walked in on a wave of excitement. They looked more kaleidoscopic than usual, so much so that I could not discern where one colour ended and the other began. Although it was autumn, they looked like spring. Spotting Anita amongst them filled my heart with joy. I was happy she was back.

I remember Gita hopping from one foot to the other, her body language bursting with news. Sita kept placing her index finger onto her lips, trying to shush her. I stood up from my teacher's chair, picked up the bouquet of kanak champas to reward them, ready to embrace their excitement.

"Didi, you knows, you knows?" Gita could not be contained.

This once, for a change, she was the one who wanted to tell me the news.

Sita beat her to it, as usual. "Anita *didded* it!"

"Did what?" My penchant for accuracy was stifled in the pride I felt knowing that Anita was the one who stood up for herself and had finally shown the courage to postpone her marriage until she was eighteen. Now Amma would realize that I had taught my girls more than their alphabet.

"I signed my name on the cerfitiket, didi!" Anita butted in, not wanting anyone to steal her thunder.

"Signed your name on which certificate?" I corrected her purely out of habit.

"Cerfitiket that says I am eighteen!" She glowed like the child-bride she was.

I remember staring at the three girls after that like I didn't know them. The yellow kanak champas fell in a heap around my feet, their delicate yellow petals astray.

"But…" I said.

"By winter I will have my own home," said Anita. "Thank you, didi…" she added belatedly.

In slow motion, I picked up my blue pilot pen that had rolled down the floor with the flowers.

Deliberately averting my gaze from their cherubic faces, I turned the cap of the pen slowly around, found the last few pages of my application forms and hastily signed my name.

Vandana Nair grew up in India, believing that relationships need to be nurtured from their roots. Living away from her birth country has given her the essential distance to mine stories from her cultural home and heritage. Movements across geographies have enabled her to complete her undergraduate degree in India, work as a freelance writer, and attain an MFA from Pacific Lutheran University's Rainier Writing Workshop.

Nair's debut novel is *Punch*, and one of her essays, *How my mother taught me to make pickles*, has been converted into a 25 minutes short Hindi language film called *Achaar*. Besides receiving an Honorable Jury mention at the 10th Kolkata Shorts International Film Festival-2021, *Achaar* was officially selected for the Indo French International Film Festival, Golden Sparrow International Film Festival, and Best Istanbul Film Festival. She lives in Washington State with her husband and two youngsters, one of whom is a canine.

ABOUT THE EDITOR

Devon Field is a writer, podcaster, and storyteller who lives in Vancouver, BC, where he teaches English to smallish children and creates the history podcast Human Circus: Journeys in the Medieval World. He is also a regular contributor to the Twilight Histories podcast. You can find him on Twitter at @circus_human.